SPECIAL FORCES

BEAR SHIFTER MATE

JADE ALTERS

JULIE

Heavy gusts of wind whipped the hull of my floatplane. An incoming snowstorm threatened to lower visibility to zero.

I wasn't turning back. Flying in Alaska was rarely easy.

I wasn't interested in easy.

I wanted out of this city and into the sky. I gripped the steering yoke and accelerated for take- off. "Good riddance, Anchorage."

I checked the controls and set my flight destination to Fairbanks where the weather was clear. For now. Late spring storms always brought a little adventure with them.

A call buzzed my phone. A photo of my grandmother appeared, requesting a video chat. I hit the button to accept. Several faces jammed onto the screen, all talking at once. None of their words were intelligible.

I knew how this conversation would go. "Hi everyone. Yes, I'm going to be careful." I waved at the toddler who grabbed the phone away from my grandmother. "I'm sorry I'm missing the drum festival." I blew a kiss at the screen. "Yes. I'll hurry back. Gotta go."

I disconnected the call to focus on steering as I veered into the air.

Another successful family call. I'd even managed to escape before they launched into all the reasons why I needed a man.

The members of my close-knit Inuit family weren't wild about my lack of dating. They also weren't wild about my job. In their minds, kids stuck close to home. And by home, they didn't mean the state of Alaska, they meant the neighborhood where we all lived.

Trapped inside an office, classroom, or clinic all day? Never gonna happen.

Roughly an hour later, I landed in Fairbanks. I got the mail delivered and the paperwork completed at top speed.

The guys were waiting on me.

'The guys' were a group of helicopter pilots stationed at Fort Wainwright near Fairbanks. They were part of a special task force they refused to talk about, but they loved flying like I did.

They were also hot. Very hot. I was well-aware of how gorgeous they were, but I wasn't attracted to them. Dylan had hit on me a few years back. Flattered, I'd kissed him, but there was no spark.

My mother, aunts and grandmother had been aghast. They freaked out in unison.

"No spark! Sparks don't pay the bills. Sparks don't hunt or fish. That man is a soldier. You take him up on his offer."

They didn't understand what Dylan had offered wasn't marriage, but a good time. That might have stopped their enthusiasm. Maybe. As the only single adult in my family, I was their only target until the next generation was ready to date.

Dylan's broad build, with his curly brown hair and olive skin, appealed to the general female population of Fairbanks.

He'd left us at the bar more than once to go home with a woman and he didn't have to put in much work to make it happen.

James hadn't come on to me outright, but he'd insinuated that he'd be up to hitting the sheets with me. Again, no chemistry.

His southern accent made him stand out around here, just as much as his red hair, fair skin, and toned body, so he wasn't without female company—when he decided he wanted it.

Sam was Inuit like me. He was lean with thick black hair, tan skin, and brown eyes. He hadn't hit on me at all. Probably because his family would react like mine and go into orbit if they detected that he'd looked twice at an Inuit woman. My family welcomed all in-laws, Inuit or not, but they definitely got excited when an in-law came preloaded with all the traditions and customs.

Like me, the guys valued their freedom. None of us were looking to settle down.

But if I was honest, there was one guy around here that did give me that certain spark.

I'd never talked to him. Never touched him. Our eyes had met, though. And I'd never forgotten it. Cheesy and overly dramatic, yes, but the first time I saw him years ago, electricity had moved in the air around him.

Sounds crazy?

Yep. But the guy was gorgeous, with a killer body thanks to being a special forces soldier. I didn't mention him to the guys much; I didn't want to hurt their feelings. Jace Branton was just a cut above any other guy I'd ever seen. Comparing him to others was not fair.

So yeah, I wasn't looking. But if Jace came up to me? Well. That would be a different story.

Hey Julie, it's kinda rude to fantasize about a guy you've never met when three of your best friends are standing right in front of you. Back to reality.

I gave myself a mental kick and smiled big at my guys.

James dropped his arm over my shoulders. "Julie! We're going to Timber Ridge Bar!"

We went there nearly every week. Their enthusiasm never dampened. I was glad to see the crew, but I wanted to get back in the air as soon as my plane was loaded. While I was in Wales, I planned to hike the National Preserve. Maybe I'd even squeeze in some cross-country skiing. "Guys, I need to get moving."

Dylan gave me a steady grin. "You can take a break."

Sam took my backpack and threw it over his shoulder. "Yeah. We're off duty, and we want to get the hell out of here." Sam tugged on my arm. "We'll buy you some cheese fries."

I laughed. "You're gonna have to try harder than that."

"We'll throw in the Italian cream cake."

"Sold." I was often in remote areas, so when I was in town, I enjoyed my food.

Dylan and James sat in the back of Sam's jeep. I climbed in the front with Sam. While the guys argued over which satellite sports channel was the best, I studied the list of best hiking areas in the National Reserve.

My planning was interrupted when we arrived at the Timber Ridge Bar in Solstice. A cozy mix of grimy bar and decent steakhouse, it was packed, but we got in within fifteen minutes.

The guys got a round of beers and I stuck with Coke.

Once the fries were delivered, we were so busy eating that no one spoke until Dylan dropped his phone on the table with a loud clunk. "Shit."

I pulled a half-eaten fry from my mouth. "What is it?"

Dylan's eyes stayed glued to his phone. "Storm's coming. Big one."

I pulled up my app. We were all trained to watch the weather. "There wasn't anything in this area on the radar when I left Anchorage. It was all down south."

He pointed a fry at me. "It's newly formed. Moving fast."

James put his beer down and frowned at me. "Jules, you better stay put. I wouldn't go to Wales. Storm's coming in from that direction."

"No way. If I wait, I'll end up snowed in here for a week with you losers. "

Dylan refilled his beer from the pitcher. "Wales is the ass-end of nowhere. They'll be fine without mail. They're used to roughing it."

I rolled my eyes at him. "Guys, you know I love you, but I have enough brothers. I don't need any more."

I wouldn't be waiting it out. If I stayed, I'd be climbing the walls.

I calculated the time it would take me to get there versus how fast the storm was developing.

I could beat this.

JACE

The bar was packed.

Damn it. Too many people, but I craved the steak that Timber Ridge Bar served. It was one of the few places that left the meat as rare as I liked it.

My bear liked raw meat. He preferred to hunt and eat deer, squirrels and rabbits, but when I was on base, I had to settle for slightly cooked.

The bar was full of soldiers from the base. Human soldiers. Not shifters. For years they'd been trying to talk to me.

There was no point.

I walked past them without stopping. Solitude was the reason I'd asked to be stationed in Alaska. They did not take the hint. One of them waved at me. "Branton! Come have a beer."

I kept walking.

They had the woman with them again today.

Julie Teslo.

She wasn't military, but she was a pilot. She flew a flimsy

little seaplane all over the state, covering military bases and the customs outpost.

My bear wasn't wild about that. It wanted her safe, not taking risks.

But since we hadn't so much as said hello, it wasn't my business.

I'd made the decision to join the Special Forces shifter unit and I knew what that meant. I'd left my clan and my family to live a bachelor's life and I was sticking to it. The only person I regularly kept in touch with was Luke, my cousin in Arkansas who also used to be in Special Forces. Sometimes I needed to talk to someone who understood but wasn't in the thick of it anymore.

The only empty table was very close to Julie's. The server was prompt and showed up quickly even with the crowd. "Will anyone else be joining you?"

"No." A server asked me that question every time I ate here. No one had ever joined me. I planned to keep it that way. "I'll take a ribeye steak. Very rare. And water."

I took the seat facing Julie.

She caught my eye the first time I'd ever seen her, years ago.

She was striking, with shiny black hair, smooth skin, and dark brown eyes. She had a small frame, and a toned, fit body. Her backside filled out her jeans perfectly, and her small round breasts were visible under her sweater.

They looked like a perfect handful each. When I was alone at home, I thought about the way her pert ass would feel in my hands. Or the way her olive skin would look laid out across my black sheets. I laid my napkin over my lap.

I never failed to get hard when I saw her.

As gorgeous as she was, that wasn't the reason I noticed her.

Her smile always got me. When she smiled, it showed all

over her face. Her eyes lit up, her dimples appeared, and she tilted her head to one side.

She was always with the soldiers, but she didn't seem to be dating any of them. Her interactions with them, as far as I could tell, were those of a friend.

It didn't matter if she was dating one of them. Or even if she was married to one of them. She wasn't mine.

We would never be together.

My bear did not like that idea at all. He wanted her to belong to me. I liked watching her move; she moved with confidence, like she knew what she wanted and how she was going to get it.

None of that mattered. She was human. I was part bear. It would never be possible.

The server placed my steak in front of me. If meat had to be cooked, then this steak looked perfect, exactly as I wanted it.

I savored the aroma of butter, garlic, and salt mixed with the scent of a rare ribeye.

I looked at Julie.

Shit. She was looking right at me.

As usual, her eyes were bright. She smiled her lovely smile. This time it was directed at me.

My bear wanted to grab her and take her to my cabin so we could be alone. I wanted her body below mine so I could possess her. So I could stare down at her beautiful face and her dark pretty eyes. But that was ludicrous. And wrong too...unless she wanted it.

I had no idea what she wanted because I'd never spoken to her.

And I wouldn't. She was human.

I was not.

I was proud to be a shifter, but I often ran on instinct. I

didn't always think like a human. And she was so small and delicate. She was probably a foot shorter than I was.

I'd been with women before. Always anonymous, always short-term. I wouldn't risk hurting them. I wouldn't risk them learning anything about my bear.

It was all so fucking complicated. We shifters weren't allowed to date humans. If we did, we weren't allowed to tell them about our true nature. If we wanted to marry a human and let them in on our secret, we needed permission from a clan elder.

Even permission didn't make you safe. Permission didn't mean humans wouldn't turn on you.

If you spend enough time with someone, the little quirks show up. A partner would take note. A partner might tell someone else.

And that someone else might expose my special forces unit. Or that someone else might kill me or the shifters in my unit.

It had happened before. Twenty years ago, a wolf shifter from another special ops group had been murdered by his girlfriend's father who'd been aghast when he found out his daughter was sleeping with a shifter. He hadn't bothered to talk to the shifter.

He only saw the animal.

The father hadn't bothered to find out that the soldier wasn't a mindless animal while in wolf form, but a highly trained member of the armed forces who loved his girlfriend.

The father had handcuffed him to a chair inside their barn and set the barn on fire. Wolves can survive a lot, but not that.

Not wanting to expose other shifters, the army kept it quiet. His murderer went free.

Faced with being shunned by her village, the girlfriend stood by her father.

After that tragedy, the shifter community took action and formalized a set of strict rules. Now, clans, tribes, and packs forbid their members to marry a human without permission. We can date, but if the relationship becomes long term, the clan will intervene. If we want to marry and reproduce, the elders must investigate both the shifter and the human.

I was glad someone took action and tried to help the unwitting shifters who often did fall in love with humans, but no. Not for me.

No way would I allow that level of scrutiny into my life.

Short hook-ups were all I had. And the last one had been a year ago. It was easier that way. Spending time with a woman might put me and my special ops unit at risk. But it was even more likely that I'd get comfortable with a human, she'd get comfortable with me, and I'd get careless.

Then she'd get hurt, or worse.

That was assuming the human I dated accepted the bear part of me.

There were scads of stories about humans who'd rejected their mates the moment they discovered the truth. It happened to my cousin. The clan elders granted him permission to marry a human woman and thereby show her his bear.

The woman was disgusted. She said he was an animal and it would be bestiality to touch him again. She'd immediately filed a restraining order.

My bear crowded at my senses.

Julie's different. I can tell.

I scoffed. Bear instincts were finely tuned. They were good for a lot of stuff. But that? Not a fucking chance. A bear couldn't know if someone was honest or not.

Humans got scared.

They did stupid shit.

I fixed my eyes back on my plate. Before I could cut into

my steak, a menu flapped in the air close to my face.

I bit back a growl.

The same soldier was talking to me again. "Man! Come on. You're off duty! Try this new beer. It tastes like—"

My phone rang. It was my commanding officer. The soldier was wrong. Unlike him, I was always on the clock. My duty to my special ops unit and to my country was paramount. It came before trivial things like tasting beer and hanging out with friends. I knew what I was getting into when I took the oath. There were some tasks that shifters just did better.

And I was glad to get some distance from Julie. She was a distraction I didn't need right now.

I'd never have a mate, but I had my job.

I nodded at my phone. "Work call."

The guys grumbled but they shut up. Julie watched as I walked past her table.

"Branton here."

I stepped outside and made my way into the empty field by the restaurant.

"Are you somewhere secure?"

"Just stepped outside of a restaurant." Eager for a mission, I pulled a black device from my bag. "I've got my jammer on. I'm ready."

"We've got a situation. According to some chatter we've picked up, a Russian sleeper cell of spies has been activated."

Fucking spies. The steak I'd craved so badly sat uneaten inside the restaurant. I was primed for a mission, but I wanted to eat too. "Where do you need me?"

"We want you to sniff around and see if you can find out who they are. Start at the border of Russia and Alaska, near Wales. The intel pins them as close to Wales."

A renewed sense of purpose pulsed through my veins. I

preferred a tough mission over idle time, any time, day or night. "Understood."

"Can you leave tonight?"

"Yes, sir." I had to get moving. I needed supplies. That was the reason I'd been in town in the first place. I'd also need to stop by my cabin.

I went back inside. I paid. I retrieved the steak. I kept my eyes forward and didn't look at the table where Julie sat.

Even without looking at her, I knew what I'd dream of tonight. Julie's tight, luscious backside naked in my shower. Her sweet, smiling face gazing up at me. And her small, feminine hands on my body.

Her eyes followed me.

I was going to have to quit running into Julie in town. Eventually, I might relax enough to say hello.

What's so scary about that?

Plenty.

I didn't need romantic turmoil in my life. My life was physically dangerous. I was heading to the border to deal with criminals. Julie was human. Breakable. A civilian. Keeping her safe was more important than what I wanted.

After his phone call, Jace Branton walked back inside the bar and laid a wad of cash on the table.

He didn't wait for a bag or container; he picked up his steak in a napkin.

Then he left.

James flipped him off but he never looked in our direction.

I was bummed. Jace was beyond handsome. He was tall, broad, and looked like he could pull a tree down with his bare hands. His green eyes stood out against his tan skin. His bone structure would qualify him as a model and those sharp cheekbones were paired with a masculine jawline. The combo made him devastatingly sexy. A jagged scar crossed his neck. He looked rugged but unapproachable.

His voice was deep, but the only time I'd heard it was when he was ordering food.

He was head and shoulders above any guy I'd seen before.

His looks were a definite plus, but that wasn't what caught my attention. His military bearing and his quiet reserve made him stand out.

So many guys around here were full of bluster and false bravado. They showed off, often with imaginary skills, and they expected any woman they approached to fall in line.

Not Jace.

He kept to himself, despite our repeated invitations.

I wanted him.

But he wouldn't play ball.

He wouldn't even come near the bleachers.

I didn't scare easily. I liked going after what I wanted. But with Jace, I steered clear. I'd wait until he made the first move.

Looked like I'd be waiting until hell froze over.

It's a stupid crush, Julie. Get over yourself. It was clear to me that my year-long dry spell was starting to wear me down.

It was just as well that he'd left. I had to get back to my plane and get to the border.

I finished the last bite of my BLT sandwich and asked for a Coke to go while my friends squabbled over the onion rings.

Sam leaned in like he had a secret to tell. "Branton came over here last week. Said hi."

My face heated. I hoped it didn't show. "Bullshit."

Sam nodded. "You like him."

"I don't know him." I wanted to. I wanted to know him in so many different ways. I liked men, but I didn't spend a lot of time picturing them naked. Not so with Jace. I pictured him naked all the time, among other things.

I wanted to peel the shirt from his strong chest and run my hands across what had to be a six-pack of cut abs. Then I wanted to unbutton his pants and—

Dylan interrupted my train of thought. "Didn't stop you from checking out his ass."

I wouldn't deny that. "Guilty as charged."

Sam elbowed Dylan. "If Jace Branton is Julie's standard, no wonder she shot you down."

James chimed in. "Yeah, he acts older than five."

The guys chuckled as I watched Jace get into his jeep. "Poor guy didn't get to eat his food."

James scooted closer to me and peered into the parking lot. "Must have been important."

"He's special forces, but never says which one," Sam said, lowering his voice. "Probably Rangers."

James threw his napkin at Sam. "Dude. You don't have to whisper. It's not a state secret."

Sam tossed the napkin back, and this time it landed in James's beer, which caused a small scuffle.

Dylan inched his chair away from Sam, who was trying to hook his leg under James's. Dylan shook his head. "Could be CIA, but deep undercover."

"Maybe." Sam shrugged. "Those guys keep to themselves."

"That certainly describes Jace." I wasn't the only one intrigued by Jace Branton, although our reasons were very different.

I piled my napkins onto my empty plate and pushed my chair back.

Sam pressed his lips together. "You're leaving, aren't you?" He crossed his arms over his chest. "Be careful."

I hugged each of them goodbye. "I always am."

I was ready to get back in the air and make my way to the border. Maybe I'd even see Jace while I was there.

I went through the pre-flight checks with Jace on my mind. Damn, that man was hot. I'd thought Dylan, James, and Sam were good-looking, but Jace was another league altogether.

All he'd had to do was walk through a public place and I was ready to hop in bed with him, along with every other woman in the restaurant.

It irritated me. I liked to think I was an independent woman, clear-headed when it came to men.

I'd watched too many of my people sabotage their own lives by making bad decisions. I loved my Inuit heritage fiercely, and the family that came along with it, but not all of them valued Western education. Some wanted to go back to the old ways. Which meant a very limited set of skills.

Flying a plane for the United States Postal Service was most certainly not included in that skill set. Nor were some of the more adventurous sports I preferred, which included solitary camping, hiking, or skiing.

Who was I to say they were wrong? I just wasn't willing to participate in their traditional formula of partnering up, having babies, and living off the land. I wasn't willing to settle for any man who'd have me.

Until I met a man that respected my desire to fly a plane and explore the outdoors when and how I wanted, I'd have to settle with the occasional hook-up.

So far, I had not yet met a man that made me second-guess my decision to stay single.

An inconvenient crush was not part of my plans.

Maybe I should have taken Dylan up on his offer. It was too late now. We were firmly in the friend-zone.

Jace would never be in the friend-zone, at least not on my end. There was no way to ignore that raw sexuality that he exuded. Any female friend of his who was interested in men would find herself permanently frustrated.

Maybe that was just me.

The truth was I'd take Jace any way I could get him.

One night stand? Check.

Friends with benefits? Check.

Relationship with commitment? Double check.

Get a grip. You are not allowed to let a man rattle you like this.

I gulped down an energy drink as a distraction.

I kept an eye on my weather radar, but the skies were clear. After a long flight, I landed easily in Wales.

Where the hell was Dimitri? The Russian customs agent should be out here helping me. He wasn't the most hearty guy in the world though; he was kind of puny. Maybe he'd taken off with the storm looming. I unloaded the mail by myself.

On to the paperwork. I marched into the building, ready to mock Dimitri's lazy ass.

The front desk area was vacant. Dimitri had really fallen down on the job. But I knew what needed to be done, so I pulled out my tablet and got started slogging through the paperwork.

The silence echoed. Dimitri usually kept the history channel running on a loop. He loved repeating the facts he'd learned.

After a few minutes of silence, I heard low murmurs from the other room. I squinted as if that would make me hear better.

Had someone turned on the television?

No. That was whispering.

It was several people. On a busy day, like Christmas, Dimitri might have one other agent with him, but not more.

I stepped around the desk toward the office. I tucked my hand into the interior pocket of my parka. Good. My knife was tucked inside. Accustomed to being alone in the wilderness, I carried a sharp hunting knife.

I slid it from the leather case and pulled it from my coat. I gripped the handle.

The whispers grew louder. The words harsher, more rapid.

Shouldn't Dimitri be trying to secure the windows and the vehicles instead of standing inside whispering?

I stepped around the corner to the sorting room.

The room was full of men.

Four stood at the counter. They weren't sorting, scanning or shredding. The men took photos, not with their approved government devices but with personal smartphones.

I took a step closer, still clutching my knife

Two more men bent over a crate near the back of the room.

The crate was full, but not with mail.

One of them reached in and pulled out an assault rifle.

Oh, fuck no. This is not simple theft. This is smuggling. Dimitri is a crook or a terrorist.

Acid rose in my throat.

I'd worked with Dimitri for years. I brought him jars of wild salmon when my family canned. He brought me books on wilderness survival.

Dimitri was a fucking snake.

I had to get out.

No way was I telling the local sheriff. He could be in on it. They'd probably bribed and threatened the local law enforcement. The invasion could be widespread.

Once I was out of there, I'd call the Coast Guard. I'd call James, Dylan, and Sam. They'd make sure this got pushed up the chain of command within the Army as far as it needed to go.

I took a careful step backward. My knife was in hand, but it wouldn't be enough. Not against six men armed with heavy weapons.

I backed up. One step at a time. I could get out. I could get back in my plane.

Just as I reached the doorway, my boot knocked into something.

I froze.

Dimitri dropped the paper he was holding.

"Julie," he said. He didn't sound shocked to see me. He was calm. Which meant he wasn't afraid of what I might do.

That was a really bad sign.

He straightened. "How very lovely to see you."

I would play dumb. It might not fly, but it could buy me some time. "Dimitri. Lovely to see you too. You didn't come out when I landed." I gave him a really big smile. "Working overtime?"

"Julie. Come. Be seated."

Like hell. "Did the government increase funding for the outpost so you could hire all this extra help?" I put my left hand on my hip, tucking the knife behind my palm. "I would've asked for a raise instead."

The six men stared at me. None spoke.

I recognized another man. Ivan. That was his name. He'd worked here as an agent during the busiest time of the year. Another measly little guy. I guess they'd taken their undercover work to heart. I obviously shouldn't criticize; they'd fooled me.

Dimitri began to pull off the gloves he was wearing.

"So nice to see you all!" I lifted my left hand in a wave. "I'll be going now. Gotta finish my paperwork."

"Julie." Dimitri's rough tone jarred me. "You will not be leaving." His mouth curled into a snarl. "We are going to be spending quality time together."

No. We most certainly are not, you sleazy prick!

I hurled the knife. Hard. Fast. Just like my grandfather taught me. Those hours in front of a target paid off. It lodged in Ivan's shoulder. Right in the softest place where the socket met his arm.

His wail echoed through the room. He hit the floor.

Dimitri leapt forward. He shoved himself around the counter. He knocked a stool over. It clattered against the concrete floor.

I ran.

JULIE

 raced from the building. Back in the cockpit, I yanked on the controls with one hand. I got the plane moving. I dialed Dylan's number. No answer.

I tried Sam. No answer.

Then James. Same thing.

I exhaled. I'd made it into the air. Visibility sucked. I was low on fuel, but I'd left Dimitri and his gang behind.

I tried my boss. Voicemail. I had to get away from Wales. The plane swooped. The fuel needle fell, faster than I'd anticipated. Keeping the plane in the air took all my strength.

An image of Jace's handsome face crossed my mind. Jace was high-level military. If I'd had his number, I'd have dialed it. It was a stupid thing to think about while running for my life, but if I didn't make it through this, I hoped Jace would find a way to be happy one day.

I regretted that I'd never had a chance with him.

I had an inexplicable feeling that he'd have been worth the work of navigating a relationship. Even for me.

Enough about a man you don't know, no matter how enticing he is. Focus.

I needed water to land. I coasted, relying on the violent bursts of wind to push the plane forward. I'd made it a few miles away from the outpost; it was far enough to evade Dimitri.

I sat up straighter. *There.* A lake, not yet covered in ice. A perfect place to land.

Close by sat a route that loggers used for trucking. I could find help once I was on the ground. I circled back around, confident in my choice.

I guided the plane down. I grasped the controls as the plane bucked in the turbulent air.

The plane jerked. It threw me backward against my seat. My seatbelts dug into my chest. My head knocked into the headrest.

Something hit me.

There were no other aircraft around. I screamed as it happened again.

I pressed my face against the cold glass of the window. Dimitri. He had followed me in one of the government-issued jeeps. He stood on the hood, holding a sniper's rifle.

He'd just shot my plane.

Dimitri had shot a fucking bullet into my plane. While I was flying it.

He'd played the part of mild-mannered weenie well. In reality, the man was a skilled sniper who was eager to murder me to protect his secret.

If I'd had another knife, I'd have hurled it at him. Never mind that it was physically impossible for it to reach him.

I yanked at the yoke. If I couldn't stab him, I could hit him with the plane. I aimed it in his direction. I pushed the gas. "I hope you die, you fucking traitor!"

Dimitri leaped from the roof of his jeep and busted his ass in the snow.

Sneaky little fucker was probably too evil to be dead.

Satisfied with my aim, I yanked tight on my seatbelt. I put both hands on the yoke and held fast. If I could maneuver just right, I might just survive this crash.

My plane plummeted.

Not far from the lake, a large grizzly bear raced along the treeline. The plane must have spooked him. If I made it past the impact, I'd have to face a bear on top of the Russian spies.

I pictured my family saying, *so Julie, how's that flying career working out for you? Wouldn't you like to move home and find a nice man to make a grandbaby with?*

The last thing I remembered was the pristine white snow drifting by.

JACE

*A*bove me, a small plane jerked sideways in the sky. It skimmed the edge of the lake, then crashed into the snowy bank.

The seaplane looked exactly like the one that belonged to Julie Teslo.

I roared. My bear instincts shoved their way forward. *You should have protected her. If you'd been with her, she'd have been safe.*

It wasn't rational.

I hadn't known Julie would be here in Wales. If I had, I would have made sure I'd tailed her, in human form, so I could keep an eye on her.

My bear didn't give a shit about my excuses.

He didn't care that the human side of me didn't want an unpleasant and messy connection to another human. He didn't care that my family and my coworkers would reject our relationship. He didn't care that true intimacy with a human would put my life in danger.

My bear had connected with Julie without asking for my permission. He saw a spark inside her and he wanted her.

There was no reasoning with him.

I'd have rescued any human from a plane crash. But I'd have been calm. Dispassionate. Focused on my task.

Thanks to my bear's apparent kinship with Julie, my instincts moved into overdrive. My bear went nuts, running fast, not watching the road, not taking care, not staying hidden.

Only one thing mattered and that was her.

Protect, protect, protect.

Why her? Why now? I didn't appreciate this disruption to my ordered life. Emotion didn't factor into a special ops soldier's life. At least not mine.

Stop thinking, dumbass. You're a soldier. Go get her.

I would not let Julie die.

I raced ahead, still in my bear form. I'd shifted to travel to Wales because it gave my bear a chance to hone his skills and the long runs kept him from getting edgy. I sent my supplies ahead on one of the special forces transports. I had nothing with me, not even clothes.

I pushed myself, snow flying up around me as I ran, the thud of my heart all I could hear. I skidded to a stop.

The plane was in pieces.

The landing gear floated in the lake. The nose of the plane was buried in the bank. The hull lay in the snow on its side.

I scented the air. If she fell in the water, her chance of survival was low. I would find her. If she were in the water, I'd dive in and get her out.

Even through the twisted metal of the cockpit, I detected the citrus scent I associated with Julie. The door was crushed inward.

I ripped the door from the plane.

There she was, unconscious, but alive. A cut slashed across her forehead. Blood dripped from the wound.

Julie had a reputation for being the most reliable mail

carrier in the state. Everyone knew she loved this little plane. She wouldn't jeopardize it.

Over the wind, I heard shouted words. I cocked my head.

Those weren't English words. The shouting was in Russian.

A bullet pinged against the metal of the plane.

I jerked my head around.

The spy cell.

These Russians were *my* assignment. They were the reason I was here.

Another bullet whizzed past my shoulder and lodged itself into the hull.

They'd attacked Julie. These professionally trained spies, who were conditioned to endure hardship, torture, and hostile conditions, had targeted a civilian. An unarmed female civilian who was fleeing.

Julie.

They'd shot her from the sky.

A seething rage rattled my bear. I bared my teeth. My blood churned, pumping through my body, fueling my fury.

All five-hundred pounds of me was primed for attack.

But first, I had to get her out.

It was much harder to hide while I was this large. We'd have to run.

I scooped her up with my massive paws. I wanted to cradle her to my chest, where she'd be warmer, but I couldn't move as quickly like that. I put her over my shoulder as carefully as I could and took off.

The shouts grew louder.

I glanced back to see the group of Russian men— six of them—chasing us with rifles.

Still grappling with the fact that this was the spy ring I'd been sent to find, I pushed myself to run harder. My legs never tired as a bear, but today, I strained my muscles until they burned hot.

My comfort was not a factor.

These spies, dangerous men, were after Julie. She'd been trying to escape from them, and she'd crashed her plane.

Killer instinct and rage rolled over me, burning through my body. I could loop back around. I could dodge their bullets, slice into their skin, rip their traitorous bodies apart, piece by piece.

But, I couldn't put her down. That would land her in more danger. My speed as a shifter was faster than a jeep out here on these rural back roads. I tried to be careful because of Julie's injuries, but I didn't slow down.

I continued to push myself to the limit. Nothing would happen to her if I could help it.

Once we were miles ahead of the spies, I stopped to check her injuries. It wouldn't do me any good to save her if she bled to death.

I leaned her against a tree and on top of a fallen log to minimize her contact with the snow. There was no blood coming from her mouth, nose, or ears. The cut on her forehead was deep, but the blood dripped in a sluggish trickle. It could wait.

The odds were six to one. I needed to plan before I took on the Russians.

I had a safehouse outside Wales, buried deep in the woods. I'd take her there.

JACE

My safehouse was a welcome sight. I'd built it myself.

It was three-hundred square feet of wood, stocked with non-perishable food, weapons, first aid supplies, and a wood-burning stove.

I lumbered up the stairs and yanked the door open. We didn't have long to linger here. After I got Julie warmed up and had a chance to look at the cut on her head, we'd leave for the next safehouse.

The Russians would track us. It would take them several hours to find this cabin, but I wanted a long head start.

Based on the way the air moved, we only had a few hours. Then the storm would pound us. Once the blizzard started, I'd keep Julie inside. I would not take a chance with her being caught out in the storm; that would be as deadly for her as any Russian spy.

I lay Julie on one of the cots.

I checked her clothes. They were mostly dry, with just a few wet spots where snow had fallen from the trees. The outside of her parka was wet, but I'd leave it on until I got the fire started.

I had been running hard for hours, yet there was no time to rest.

I tugged on a dresser drawer with my paw. I didn't want Julie to wake up alone in a remote cabin with a naked man. That wouldn't do her head wound any favors.

A sharp intake of breath sounded behind me.

I spun around.

Julie was awake.

She sat up on the cot, with her back pressed against the wall. Her mouth opened. Her hands clenched around the edge of the cot. Her face paled.

Shit.

In trying to avoid being naked, I hadn't thought about her seeing my hulking grizzly bear. Revealing ourselves to humans was expressly forbidden, by both my shifter clan and my special ops unit. My commanding officer would be happy to rip me a new one. And he'd be right to do so. If I hadn't been so damn distracted by having Julie in my space, I could have easily stepped outside to shift.

My CO wouldn't sympathize with my reasoning. Not for a second. Nor would my parents, or my grandparents. Not shifting in front of humans was a basic lesson we learned as children. There were no excuses.

Again, I'd let my emotions toward Julie control my actions.

I shifted.

It didn't take long, just a few seconds, and then I looked like Jace again, the guy she'd seen in Fairbanks at the bar.

She screamed. It wasn't a long scream. She cut herself off and let go of the cot. She pressed her hands to her face. Her shoulders shook. Big sobs rattled her small frame. Blood seeped through her left fingers and made a trail down her face.

It dripped down onto her coat, staining it a deep mahogany color.

Those freaks had caused her to bleed.

I pulled on a pair of track pants and a t-shirt. Everything in me wanted to comfort her, but I didn't want to upset her more. I could at least get her warm. Maybe that would help.

I tossed several pieces of firewood into the stove and stuffed some newspaper in the holes. I lit a match; the flame ignited. The room would heat up soon.

She'd dropped her hands. Her face was smeared with blood. She wasn't sobbing but just making little hiccuping sounds. It had to be hurting her head.

My bear didn't like it.

I crossed the room. I pulled her into my arms.

She didn't resist. She threw her arms around my neck. She laid her head on my shoulder. I hated to see her in pain, but I was grateful she was letting me hold her. She felt right in my arms. I inhaled, savoring her one-of-a-kind scent: Julie, mixed with citrus. Even her hair smelled like lemons.

Having her in my arms was what my bear had wanted for a long time.

What if I hadn't been in the woods at the moment she crashed?

What would the Russians have done to her? Familiar with their spy training programs, I shuddered to think of what they'd have in store for her, especially if she had intel they wanted. If I spent too long considering the possibilities, my bear would go crazy.

I would kill all six of them. Each of them would die for taking down her plane. No defense would be enough.

My orders did not involve killing the spies. But in my

special forces shifter group, we had the leeway to make the tough decisions.

I would make this one. If I let them live, Julie would never be safe. From an American prison cell, the spies could continue to hunt her, to hurt her. As long as one of these vile Russian spies breathed air, there was always a chance of them coming after her.

I held her close until her body began to feel warmer. Her trembling subsided. She sighed and her entire body sagged.

I did not want to disturb her, but I wanted to clean the cut on her head. Shifters were blessed with genetics that meant we healed fairly quickly, but humans were not. Humans were also prone to infection.

I leaned back a little. "I'm going to look at this cut."

She started to nod, then grimaced. "Ow."

I would have gladly traded places with her.

The cut was deep. It needed stitches, but we'd have to get by with some butterfly bandages and tape. It also needed to be cleaned with an antiseptic.

I grabbed the first aid kit. I wiped my hands down with rubbing alcohol, then I poured some on a cotton pad. "This is going to sting."

She gazed up at me with her dark brown eyes. They still looked a little unfocused but she flattened her mouth into a straight line. "I routinely camp outside in Alaska. A little rubbing alcohol won't bother me. Go for it," she said.

My eyebrows shot up at her sass.

My bear liked it. My bear liked a woman who didn't shy away from the hard things in life.

I dabbed at the cut. She flinched but didn't pull away. I cleaned as much of the blood off as I could. I pasted the bandage strips across the cut. When I was in the field with the other bear shifters, we slapped bandages on without a lot of care. But this was a woman's face, and I didn't want to be that haphazard with a potential scar.

I knew from my own scar that people would stare and ask questions. The scar that crossed my neck came from a real bear, in a freak accident. Most people assumed it came from my military service. I'd had a few women—women who actively pursued me for a date—ask me if I was stabbed in prison.

Stabbed in prison? Was that the kind of vibe I gave off?

My fellow soldiers had howled with laughter that night. They found it hilarious that I looked scary.

I didn't think it was all that funny. But for me, it could be useful. Looking scary as a special forces soldier in the army? Helpful more often than not.

For a female pilot like Julie?

Probably not as much.

I didn't want to be the cause of that kind of attention for her.

I put the kit back together and placed it on the table. I crouched in front of her. "Look at me." Her eyes met mine. I wished I were staring into them for a different reason, instead of checking for brain damage. "Your pupils are the same size. That's a good sign. Are you dizzy at all?"

"A little."

"Nauseated?"

"Some."

"Headache?"

"Yes."

"You probably have a mild concussion. I'll get you some Tylenol. Let's get this coat off."

She lifted one arm and began to shrug out of the coat, but it didn't come all the way off. Her movements were stiff as I helped her tug at it.

"Any pain while doing that?"

"No."

"I need to touch your ribs. Is that okay?"

Once she nodded, I skimmed my hands down her sides. "Take a deep breath." I watched her closely. "Hurt anywhere?"

"No. Wouldn't I notice if I had a broken rib?"

"Maybe. Maybe not. With the surge of adrenaline from an accident, sometimes it takes a while for the pain to set in."

She huffed. "I'd say being shot out of the sky and crashing my plane in the snow is a pretty big adrenaline rush. Wouldn't you?"

I stood up. My bear wanted to keep his hands on her, but the damn animal had no boundaries.

"So earlier," she said. "You were a bear. A gigantic bear."

Julie had gotten away from trained spies; she was obviously no slouch in the brains or the guts department. In addition, she'd seen me as a bear and she wasn't afraid to question me about it.

I was a pretty big human, but as a bear, I wasn't some cuddly pet. I was big, bulky and scary.

Her spicy attitude and refusal to give up were good qualities around here. She'd have made a good soldier.

I said nothing. Dread washed over me. What would she do now? Could she convince anyone else of what she'd seen?

How much had I put my team at risk?

I refused to threaten her. I'd have to convince her nicely to not reveal my secret.

"I saw you. When I was still in the plane. Before I crashed."

Shit. The second I'd seen that blasted floatplane, I'd known it was Julie. I'd lost focus and I'd lost cover. She'd obviously spotted me easily from the sky.

Would I ever regain my composure around her?

"Yes," my bear supplied. "If you take her as a mate, you'll feel much better!"

Shut up.

I doubted having her as a mate would lessen my need to protect her. It would probably make the urge worse, though I doubted that was possible.

She pursed her lips. "I know you can speak. I heard you just a second ago. That was you here in the cabin, right? The giant bear? You're not hiding a pet."

I wasn't going to lie to her, not now. She wouldn't have believed me anyway. "Yes. I'm a bear shifter."

"Jeez. What a trip." She rubbed her hands over her eyes a few times. "I can't believe it. Am I hallucinating?" Her eyes widened. "Is this a trick? You know, for one of those reality shows?" She pointed to the ceiling. "Is there a hidden camera up there?"

"No. This is real."

She glowered. "Maybe Dimitri is a snake shifter. That would fit him."

This was the first time I'd seen her without even a trace of her trademark smile. "Who is Dimitri?" Was this the name of one of the spies?

"He's a rat fucking piece of scum."

"Was he at the customs outpost?"

"Yes. He's the asshole who shot my plane. Dimitri Petrov."

Blinding fury washed through my body at the name of the man who tried to kill Julie. My heartbeat sped up, my stomach twisted. My claws extended, ready to rip flesh, my teeth sharpened, ready to bite. *No.*

I hadn't lost control of my bear since I was a teen. I would not start now, no matter how my bear felt about Julie.

I flexed my hands. I ran my tongue over my teeth until they were human again. "I'm going to guess that he's Russian?"

"He is." She coughed a few times. I hoped she wasn't getting sick on top of the head injury. She fixed her eyes on me. "All these years that I've seen you in the bar and around Alaska, you've been able to do that? Change back and forth?"

I willed my pulse to slow. I needed to question her, to find out about the spies, not let her meander down a path of inquiry about my bear. *She's not the perp here, Jace. She's the victim. Keep it straight.* As if my bear would let me forget.

"Yes."

"Is that why you don't talk to us?"

"That's part of it." It was most of it, but I didn't need to admit that.

"What's the other part?"

She didn't relent. Most of the time, if I had a romantic partner, our time together was brief. The woman took the hint and didn't push me. So far, Julie wasn't taking any hints at all. "I'm part of a special ops military unit. It's dangerous. I don't want humans involved."

"Too late, buddy. I'm in it." She made a face. "I was in it when Dimitri put a bullet in my plane."

My bear didn't like being reminded of that. He pushed at me again, wanting me to leave immediately and go after this Dimitri. However, I still had a job to do.

"I need you to focus on Dimitri right now. I found your plane crashed into the lake near the customs outpost. He shot you down?"

"Yeah. He's the Russian customs agent. We've known each other for years. He really liked the history channel." She made a fake gagging sound. "I should have known something was up from that alone. So many documentaries."

I marveled at Julie's brazen humor in the face of this shit storm. Making light was the last thing I felt like doing.

The only thing I could feel was pissed off. Pissed off that I was too late to intercept the spies at the outpost, pissed off that Julie had become a target.

She pursed her lips. "I can't wrap my head around the fact that he's a spy. He's a wimpy little guy. How can he be a spy?"

"Spies can take any shape. This infiltration was likely in the works for years. He had a role to play and he was trained well to play it, possibly for his entire life. What else?"

"They were going through mail. They were taking photos with their phones. They had a giant crate full of guns. And ammunition."

Dammit. I needed to get this intel to my CO. "How many men were with him?"

Julie scrunched her face up briefly. She rubbed her fingers over her temple. "Five, six total including him. I recognized one. His name is Ivan."

"Another customs agent?"

"Yes. Part-time. I'd never seen the other four men before."

"Perfect. Those are great observations. Were you able to contact anyone?" If she had and her call was intercepted, then the Russians might send reinforcements.

"No. I tried calling my friends in the army. I tried my boss."

Her friends. The men from the bar that she was close to. Again my bear growled. He didn't like her talking to other men.

Not your call, buddy.

"None of the calls went through," she said. Her voice sounded strained.

I'd been in those situations enough to know how nerve-wracking they were. I signed up for that kind of peril. She had not.

I had to push my bear away. Again, he insisted that we find the spies and rip them limb from limb. He didn't see the need to gather any additional information beyond the fact that they hurt Julie.

I assured him that the spies would die for what they'd done.

She tilted her head back and looked me in the eye. "What were they doing?"

"That's what I'm here to find out."

"Nice evasion, but I want to know. Are they planning an attack?"

It was possible. More likely, they were planning further infiltrations. More outposts corrupted, more agents on the ground, blending in as harmless residents until activated by the Russian government.

Julie didn't need to know all that. "You're handling this remarkably well."

"Not really. My grandfather used to take me out when I was a kid. We did survival hunts, so I've been out in these small cabins before. And the Inuits have myths about shifters. I guess they weren't myths after all." She shrugged and gave me a half-hearted smile. "I'm sure I'll freak out later."

She ran a hand through her hair. "I knew something was wrong. The television wasn't blaring. Her jaw tightened. "They fucking ruined my plane."

I didn't care about the stupid plane. I'd make sure she got another from the post office if it came to it, but all I cared about was the fact that they'd almost killed her. I wasn't going to leave her here a second longer. We were sitting ducks in this cabin. "We're moving out."

Julie's eyes narrowed. "Now?"

"We have to get to the next house before the storm sets in." I sniffed the air. "We don't have long. I can feel it."

"Are we driving?"

"I don't keep a car here. I'm going to shift and you're

going to hang on while I run." It was far from ideal but it was what we had.

"That sounds really weird."

I wasn't wild about it either. In a split second, I'd gone from never having shared my secret with a human to allowing one to ride on my back. It wasn't exactly a joyride for me either. My bear liked it though.

She's our mate, my bear crowed happily.

He needed to get a grip.

"It's what's going to happen."

I studied her pale face and drooping eyes. She probably needed food. "Are you hungry?"

She pushed herself off the cot and stood. "I'm starving."

I handed her a granola bar. "Eat that." I grabbed a few packets of dried fruit and beef jerky and stuffed them in one of the pockets of a coat I kept in the cabin. "These are in case of emergency. We'll eat when we get to the next safehouse."

I held the coat up. "Wear this. It's the newest technology and will keep you warmer." Once she'd swallowed the granola bar, I helped her wrap up in it.

She grabbed my arm. "I threw my knife at one of the spies. That jackass probably still has it. Do you have any spares?"

My jaw dropped. "You threw a knife?" Why was I just now hearing about this? How many risks could one civilian take in a day?

"Yep. Got him right in the shoulder." Her eyebrows drew together. "I wish I'd hit him in the throat. I need to practice more."

My bear rumbled. He liked how fierce she was. I didn't like thinking of her confronting those monsters. But she was better off with a weapon than without. I collected a knife from my storage crate that would fit her hand well.

I handed it to her. My bear preened when my hand brushed over hers and she gave me a nice smile.

"Thanks." She turned the knife over in her hands. She touched the blade before putting it back in the sheath and tucking it in her pocket.

"I'm going to shift. When I do, climb on my back and hang on tight. But first I'm going to have to take these clothes off."

Julie grinned. "Do I say giddy-up?"

"I'm not a horse," I growled.

Not wanting to waste any more time, I left the clothes on the bed and shifted back into my bear.

I waited on all fours as she gingerly threw her leg over my back, then pulled all of her weight on top of me.

She clutched at my back and buried her face in my fur.

I'd expected to resent the feel of a human on my back. I didn't. Not one bit. Not if that human was Julie.

JULIE

Snow fell around us as Jace ran, glittery little bits of fluff that melted on contact. With a big storm brewing, that wouldn't be the case for long.

I hung on tight as Jace raced through the woods. I kept my face down, buried in his soft fur. His body was warm against mine and with his coat, I wasn't as cold as I'd expected to be.

What a shit storm of a day. The beginning started out fine. Talked to my family, ate with my guy friends, flew my plane.

Then I'd busted up an international spy ring. Stabbed a spy. Crashed my plane.

And the kicker: rode on a bear shifter. Who was really the hot guy I had a crush on.

Fun times.

I'd finally got my wish to see Jace naked and I'd barely had time to appreciate it. First, I'd been so stunned by the gargantuan bear roaming around the cabin to pay attention when he shifted. Then I'd been too busy averting my eyes out of respect when he shifted the second time.

Respect was overrated.

I turned my head to look behind us. Dimitri and his henchmen wouldn't give up. They hadn't spent time setting up this operation only to let it go because a mail carrier caught them. Dimitri, that little shit, had tricked me. For years.

Which was all part of Dimitri's nefarious plan, according to Jace. He could waltz into our country, work behind a counter, pretend to be a feeble bureaucrat. Then bam! Out of the blue, he transformed into an evil spy—complete with sniper skills — who shot me down.

Guys like that? They wouldn't give up.

They would continue to hunt us until they found us.

Or until Jace found them.

I was having a hard time letting it sink in that Jace was a bear. I knew spy cells were a reality. I hadn't known shifters were. Here I was gripping his fur, and it still seemed like a fairy-tale.

Apparently, the United States military had entire units made up entirely of guys like Jace. People who could shift into animals.

Unlike the werewolf lore we'd all heard, Jace was entirely himself when he was a bear. He could think, reason, and make tactical decisions.

He'd saved me from the plane wreckage when he was in his bear form. Mind-boggling didn't begin to describe it.

A tiny voice inside my head thought that maybe, just maybe, he might be worth taking a chance on.

Now is not the time to plot a potential date, Julie. You know nothing about him.

He could turn into a bear. He saved my life. Both of those should count for something.

Speaking of planes, my busted up plane pissed me off. It wasn't mine, but I lived in it. My poor seaplane was in pieces, according to Jace. I was almost glad I hadn't seen the damage.

The United States Postal Service would be less than pleased. I had a feeling the spies didn't carry insurance to replace it.

I glanced back again.

A blur flashed across the snow.

I jolted and gripped Jace's fur harder.

I sagged as I stared into the blizzard.

Just a rabbit.

Not a spy.

I needed my knife in hand. I pulled it from my coat pocket. I'd have to hold it while I hung onto Jace, but the awkward grip was worth knowing it was close by for throwing.

Another quick glance backward showed only trees. No spies.

The snow began to grow thicker. Each flake was heavier and they'd stopped melting. Visibility was low for me. I didn't know how well Jace could see like this. It didn't matter because the conditions were getting worse and we couldn't turn back now.

I tucked my face into his fur and closed my eyes. The rocking motion would have been comforting if not for my probable concussion. As it was, I was slightly nauseated, but there was nothing I could do about it.

Before long, Jace slowed to a walk. I lifted my head. He brought us to the mouth of a cave. The air coming from the cave was distinctly warmer than the air outside.

Jace slowed his pace more and we walked into the cave beyond the mouth. He stopped. I waited a few moments, wondering what he was doing before I realized he probably wanted me off his back. I lowered my left leg and then sort of slid to the ground. He crouched a little so that I didn't completely fall off and land in a heap.

My eyes adjusted to the dim light.

As soon as I stood, Jace shifted back into a man.

A smoking hot man.

Part of me was awed that after all the chaos, I could appreciate Jace's looks. It did give me a little comfort that I hadn't injured my brain past the point of caring about Jace's muscular form.

I averted my eyes while he walked toward a sealed crate, although he didn't seem to be modest. I caught a glimpse of his bare shoulders as he pulled on pants and a t-shirt.

From the back, he looked great in a pair of track pants. The fabric clung to his tight ass. Luckily for me, him being a bear meant I didn't have to imagine what he looked like with nothing on at all.

I guess he didn't get very cold. In the bar earlier, he'd had on long sleeves like everyone else.

I glanced up at the damp ceiling. "A cave? Do you hibernate?"

Jace glared at me.

I laughed. I couldn't help it. "You have a cave. Like a real bear."

"I get it."

"Do you get a lot of bear jokes?"

"No one knows except my unit. They're shifters too. So no, it's not funny."

He said that, but he didn't seem pissed.

"So, if wolf shifters are called werewolves, are you called a werebear?" I fanned my face as I snickered. "Sorry. I think I'm delirious."

He shook his head. "My CO calls us Carebears when he's mocking us during training."

He didn't laugh exactly, but he did make a small huffing

sound. Close enough. So he did have a sense of humor. Maybe it was just buried deep.

He lit several lanterns with that hung from the cave wall with a lighter.

I was struck again by how beautiful he was. I had known he was in shape, but the t-shirt showed off even more of his impressive build. I'd have been happy if he'd left the clothes off. As it stood, I wanted to put my hands all over him.

My year-long dry spell hadn't affected me—until now. Now, with Jace, I wanted to rip those clothes right back off of him and press my body up against his tan skin.

What the hell was going on with me?

I liked men, but my physical desire for them had never been so potent.

Had the crash knocked something loose in my brain? Or was it just Jace's appeal? I covered my mouth to stop a giggle and to stop myself from making a crack about animal magnetism. I didn't want to give away my desire for Jace just yet.

I found a rubber band in my pocket and pulled my hair up off my neck. I tied it in a ponytail. It was supremely nice not to be cold. "It feels good in here."

He smiled. "There's an underground hot spring. You can take a bath in the water. It's why I picked it as a safehouse. I have food here. There's a real bed when you're tired."

I was impressed. The lights gave off a warm amber glow, and the moving springs made the same bubbling noises that a creek did. After the day I'd had, it was soothing. "It's nice. Feels homey."

He ducked his head. He was so strong and tough; it was sweet to see him do something like that. I wondered if he was blushing.

"Are you hungry again?" he asked.

"A little."

"I'll get out what I have and start a fire."

I watched him stack the wood into a pile. Just like in the cabin, he stuck newspapers in the open spaces and lit a match.

"We have canned black beans and canned corn."

I was near to swooning. It wasn't a gourmet meal or a five-star restaurant, but no man had ever offered to cook for me before. "Sounds perfect. Better than muktuk."

Jace gave me a blank look.

"Whale blubber. Inuit staple." There were no picky eaters in my family. If anyone complained, we heard the stories of our ancestors living off the land, eating muktuk. We'd all had to try it as kids. "Imagine liver with fish juice poured on top. But you better believe that if my grandmother gave it to me, I choked it down." I shuddered. "You'd probably like it."

"Is that another bear reference?"

"I can't resist. It will probably never get old."

"Speak for yourself," he said. Jace opened the cans and dumped them into a cast iron pan which he stuck over the open fire.

"I can help," I said. "If you need me to do something." I wasn't used to sitting around and doing nothing.

He shook his head. "You rest. This will only take a few minutes to heat up."

He spread a thick blanket on the cave floor and we sat next to the fire.

"Speaking of families, do you think mine thinks I'm dead?"

"Do you want the real answer?"

"Always. I'd rather you be real with me than baby me."

"Yes. They'll assume you're dead. At least, the post office will. With that crash, the temps outside, and the storm, they'll assume your body is at the bottom of the lake, or that your body was carried off by animals."

"Ah." I'd wanted honest and I'd gotten it. My poor family. It made me queasy to think of the pain they'd suffer thinking I'd been killed in the plane crash. When I got back home, there'd be hell to pay. They'd never want me to fly again.

"Sorry to be so graphic."

"Nah. I'm from here too." We'd all grown up on tales of people who died because they twisted an ankle and fell into a snowdrift, never to be heard from again.

We were taught never to go out alone, but so many of us were thrill-seekers at heart that we took a chance and did it anyway.

"I know what this land does to people who screw up. You can't have accidents in the Alaskan countryside and expect to walk away, unless you have a big strong bear that just happens to be strolling by."

Jace made a face.

He made it really easy to pick at him. "I love Alaska, but it's unforgiving." I sighed. "I suppose my boss will think the same thing."

"Most likely. If you'd crashed in clear weather conditions, they'd probably send out a rescue team. Our unit has helped with search and rescue before, when appropriate. But with the circumstances of your crash, well. They probably couldn't search."

"That weasel Dimitri probably called in to report that I was drunk or high. So they won't investigate."

"This won't go on forever. I'll find him." Jace's deep voice resonated in the cave. "He won't get away with this."

As I'd said, swooning over a man was for wusses. But in that moment, I was smitten. Jace was a real-life hero.

I wanted to know more about him. It was clear he liked to stay away from humans and now he'd been forced into having one in his home.

He had just carried me at top speed for miles and miles

across the frozen ground. And I had fallen apart all over him. I hadn't thought much about it at the time because I'd been so muddled and freaked out, but I had cried all over him.

I wasn't much of a crier. I couldn't remember the last time I'd cried. I decided I'd blame it on the head injury, although crashing my plane and finding out Dimitri was a spy probably were both big contributors as well.

My face flushed as I remembered crawling into his lap and putting my head on his shoulder.

He'd felt so nice. Comforting. And he hadn't acted annoyed or put out. I hadn't even thought to be embarrassed at the time.

"I'm sorry I cried all over you earlier. You were patient and I appreciate it."

His bright green eyes met mine. "It's my job."

So much for a heartfelt apology.

Even though I'd have rather not fallen apart, I regretted that I hadn't been coherent enough to appreciate his holding me. I'd been pressed up against him, and in his lap, and I'd been an incoherent mess.

Not that I thought I'd had a chance with him anyway, but now I definitely didn't.

Maybe we could be friends, though. I wasn't sure how I'd stay friends with someone this deliciously hot. The urge to try and take things further would interfere with any feelings of friendship I might have.

I couldn't keep sitting there in awkward silence. "It smells good."

"It's ready." He pulled a wooden spoon and two metal plates from another crate. He scooped half onto my plate and half onto his. He handed me a metal fork as well.

I motioned to his plate. "I think you need more food than I do."

"No. Your body needs it to recover."

I could tell he wasn't going to budge. "Thank you." I took a bite. The open fire had roasted the corn and beans and added a smoky flavor. "It's delicious."

He huffed a small laugh. "The other guys in my squad think it's gross. They'd rather go find a rabbit." He ate a few big bites.

"Your squad? Are you all shifters? Must come in handy."

"We heal quickly. If those Russian spies had shot me, I'd have been able to keep going, most likely. Not true for a human."

I hated to think of him putting himself in harm's way. I barely knew him, but I wanted him safe. "Do you get shot often?"

"Occasionally."

"What? I thought you'd say no!"

I'd learned from my soldier friends at the Fairbanks base that they tended to downplay the risks they took while serving their country. "Occasionally" meant "all the damn time."

He pointed to a large scar across his neck. "I didn't get this protecting our country, although I let people assume that I did. I made the mistake of tangling with a real grizzly."

He was really good at avoiding the questions I asked. "Fuck." I had the strongest urge to reach out and touch him. But I didn't think he'd like that. "Does that happen a lot?" My stomach twisted into a small knot. Now I had to worry about him engaging with real bears as well as fighting spies?

He laughed. "No. That was an accident. One I won't repeat again."

I finished my food. He'd probably reached the limit of how much he wanted to share and I was exhausted. The hot springs were sounding better and better. "You said I could get in the water here?"

Jace took my plate. "Yes. It'll help any sore muscles you have from the crash and it'll warm you up."

"I'm definitely going to do that." I pushed myself to my feet and my legs protested. The muscles in my thighs felt like they'd been pummelled. Maybe they had. I lifted my arms over my head. Ouch. A burning ache rushed down my back. The hot water sounded better and better.

Jace coughed. "I'll give you some privacy while I check our supplies."

Heat crawled across my body at the thought of stripping in front of him. But he'd done it earlier. I was hardly going to ask him if he kept a swimsuit handy in a remote military base.

Jace moved away with stiff motions to go search under the bed.

I turned my back and began to pull my clothes off. By the time I was down to my bra and panties, every part of me was aware that there was a man in the room. A very handsome man that I'd had a crush on for years.

I undid my ponytail and shook my hair out over my shoulders. A very basic part of me wanted to parade in front of him, with my body on display. Not by accident, but by design. For him.

Would Jace look? Would he want to?

Would he want to be the one to take off my bra?

Would he want to touch me?

I had no idea. He'd given no indication that he did want those things. And he was an honorable man. He'd have saved anyone in my position. It didn't mean anything.

I unhooked my bra and put it on top of my shirt. Finally, I pushed my panties down and folded them under my pants. I moved as quickly as I dared, not wanting to slip on the rocks and bust the other side of my head open.

I stepped into the hot water.

The relief was immediate. It was so overwhelmingly good that I forgot I was naked in the same room with Jace. But just for a second.

I let my body sink to the floor of the spring. Sitting on a rock, I submerged my body all the way to my neck. Pure bliss. The only way to improve the experience would be to get Jace in here with me.

Not fucking likely. But I was going to try. Eventually.

I closed my eyes, trying to unwind some of the tension that I'd stored in my body after all the craziness of the day.

"I'm in," I called out to Jace. "It's safe to look!"

He didn't reply.

He moved around the room again, pulling out batteries and warmer blankets. I watched him, acutely aware that just feet away, I was sitting naked under the bubbling water.

JACE

*M*y bear wanted to sink his teeth into the Russians, to swipe his claws across their chests. He wanted to go slow. To break bones. To bleed them dry.

He wanted to crush their heads against stone. He wanted to throw their bodies into fire.

I had to regain some control. I took an axe from the supplies. I stood near a tree at the mouth of the cave. I drove the axe into the tree. Over and over until the tree fell. After twenty minutes, I still wanted to run off to kill the Russians, but the urgency had faded.

Beyond the anger was the desperate want for Julie. Before her, lust had been a physical urge. Now I wanted inside her body. I wanted her scent on me.

Usually, when people cried, I wanted to escape. I had no idea what to do.

But when Julie cried, all I wanted was to comfort her.

Now I wanted her back in my arms, not because she was upset. Because she wanted me to.

I had enjoyed spending time with a woman that I found

alluring. That was a first in my life. She was easy to talk to. I didn't like talking about myself, but with Julie, I didn't mind nearly as much. Her questions were curious, not invasive.

The physical attraction I felt for her was the strongest I'd ever known. My body had reacted. I'd been hard for the last thirty minutes while Julie bathed.

Knowing she was over there, naked under the water, ate at me. Touching her smooth olive skin was all I could think about. I'd had human lovers before. It was difficult to be close to them when I couldn't share such a huge part of myself with them.

Julie knew about my secret now.

It was no longer a reason to stay away. That barrier would never exist between us.

My erection throbbed. It had been a year since I'd been with a woman, and the desire I felt for Julie grew by the second.

"I'm going out to hunt. I'll stay near the cave," I said. I had to get out and cool off before I did something stupid.

"If you need to chase a squirrel, I understand," she smirked. "Ok, enough with the bear jokes."

I didn't mind at all. I was teased mercilessly by the guys in my unit, but I'd never had that kind of closeness with a woman.

The smirk slid into a sexy curve. "I can think of something better to do. Why don't you join me in the hot springs?"

Join her? My brain got stuck.

She wanted me in the water with her. While she was naked.

Get in! If our teammates were here, they'd wallop you upside the head! My bear's shout was frantic. He did not want me to screw up this opportunity.

I snuck a glance at her. She had that smile on her face that captivated me. It was so open. So inviting. In spite of what she'd been through today, she was grinning at me and showing off those dimples.

I didn't want her to feel like I was rejecting her. Not today.

I wanted this. So much that I was petrified to consider letting myself have it.

"If you're sure," I said.

She lifted her hands from the water, making a little splashing sound. "Don't bears like water?" The smirk was back; this time her lips were pouty.

My bear roared. He wanted to jump in and grab her. I pushed him back. He was getting a little too insistent.

I stripped, faster than normal. As a shifter, I had no modesty, but I didn't want to alarm Julie with my body's reaction.

I stepped into the water and lowered my body. I sat on a rock across from Julie and folded my arms across my chest. I didn't want to appear intimidating or threatening without even trying, and that was easy for me to do. I'd heard that plenty of times, from shifters and humans alike.

One woman I dated, and I use that word loosely, told me the scar on my neck made me look scary.

Bad train of thought. Move on.

I tried to relax.

It wasn't easy.

The water stirred. My eyes flew open. Julie was no longer sitting across from me on her rock. She was right in front of me.

I pressed my back against the wall of stone. She wasn't standing up straight, but the water no longer covered her up to her neck. Her collar bone was exposed, along with the top of her chest. If I looked down, I'd be able to see her round breasts right under the surface of the water.

I was the hardest I'd ever been. My cock throbbed. The need to bury it inside her body was primal.

I pushed my shoulders farther back into the stone. I would keep my hands to myself, until she said otherwise. If she gave the green light, her body would be mine.

Mine, said my bear.

Her eyes were half-closed and she no longer looked confused, or addled. She looked like a woman who knew what she wanted. And she was looking right at me.

JULIE

I never understood women who chased men. I couldn't relate. Now? Totally got it. I craved being close to Jace. The desire to touch him, to be with him, was crawling through me.

I'd never thought of sex in such crude terms, but I wanted his cock. I wanted to see it. I wanted to taste it. I wanted him to enter me in a way I'd never wanted a man to before.

What was happening to me?

Jace had saved my life.

He had been caring when I cried.

He had cooked for me when I was hungry.

All of that made for a great man, but add in his handsome face, gorgeous body, and the mystery of the bear that was always inside him, and my desire was pretty understandable. Even from a logical, objective point of view.

I didn't feel logical. Not one bit.

I considered swimming over to him and dropping onto his lap.

But no. That wouldn't be right. I needed to give him a chance to decide if he was interested.

I had finally decided that just for one night, I would let go of my inhibitions and enjoy the comfort of a man.

Or a man who was also a bear.

Somehow that made him even more attractive.

Now I only had to convince Jace, who was still sitting with his back jammed up against the stone. I'd always waited on a man to make the first move, which was advice my grandmother had given me. "Let him know you're interested, honey. But don't chase him. That's what they like to do. They like the chase," she'd said.

That advice had gotten me nowhere with Jace. He probably did like the chase, in theory. Especially if his bear called any of the shots. But he was going to deny what he wanted, because of his duty, and because of his bear. So if anything was going to happen, it was up to me.

I took a very deep, very steadying breath. My head hurt, but it was a dull ache now and not a stabbing pain now, and the cut barely twinged. I was ready.

I could do this. "I want you," I said looking right at Jace.

I could tell he was going to argue.

But he didn't seem uninterested, just worried. "In one day, you were chased by thugs, crashed a plane to survive, and you have a concussion. There's no way you're thinking straight."

"You're right. I was chased by thugs and I got away. I did crash a plane and I lived through it. I probably have a concussion, but I'm not confused. I saw you in the Timber Ridge Bar. I wanted you then."

I paused in my speech to look at Jace, whose eyebrows were raised.

"You were wearing dark jeans and a navy blue sweater that looked great with your sandy hair. The blue stood out with your green eyes too,"

Jace opened his mouth but I wasn't done. "Before you

could touch your food, you got a call, which I assume was about Dimitri and his gang, and you left to talk. You came back, grabbed your steak, and took off. I remember every detail because I watched you. I've wanted you for years but you never talk to me. You can talk to me now. You can do more than talk to me."

I had to take drastic action. I stood up. The water was below my waist now, so Jace could see my bare breasts and my stomach, all the way down to the spot between my legs which was getting more heated by the second.

I took the last few steps toward him.

Jace sat with his mouth open. His strong jaw moved a few times, but he didn't speak.

I reached out and touched him, just the tips of my fingers to his shoulder. I wanted to give him a chance to get away if he wanted.

His skin was warm. The hard muscle under my fingers jumped. All that contained strength. Just waiting for me. As I stood there, my hand lightly touching his arm. Jace's chest heaved. His breaths started coming in pants.

I realized then that he was fighting for control.

"You want me, don't you?"

He nodded.

"How much do you want me?"

"As much as I can have of you."

He was welcome to every part of me.

"Have you ever been with a woman?"

"Yes." His voice was rough. "It's been a year. I don't know how gentle I can be."

"Don't worry about that. Just relax. Uncross your arms. Let me touch you."

He drew in a deep breath and uncrossed his arms.

I wanted to take my time. It had been a long time for both

of us and it sounded like relationships had not come easily to him. I wanted to make this good.

He sat cross-legged on the rocks and I took one step closer until I was almost straddling him.

I lifted my hand to his face. I cupped his cheeks and felt along his strong jaw. The stubble on his face was rough and masculine. I leaned forward to run my hands through the back of his thick hair. The motion brought my chest closer to his mouth. His breath fanned across my nipples and they hardened.

Just his breath on my skin made me ache with desire.

What would having his hands on me do?

I moved my hands down his muscled back, enjoying the hard planes of his sculpted body.

I pulled them around to the front to feel his firm pecs.

I pushed my hands down, feeling across his flat stomach.

He gasped, inhaled a breath.

I pulled my hands back. I didn't want to move too fast. He'd waited a year to be with a woman, and even now he was reluctant to sleep with me because I was human. I wanted this to be right for him. I inched closer. Now my thighs touched his.

His hands were by his sides now, but he made no move to lift them.

I straddled him fully now, lowering myself until I was seated against him, my bare skin against his, only the warm water between us.

His arousal was hard against me. My stomach flipped over. My desire surged. The spot between my legs grew wetter. I had never in my life wanted a man like I wanted Jace.

Jace's restraint was amazing. He could have had me on my back by now and I'd have been willing. But he stayed where he was. I hoped his patience would benefit both of us.

I wrapped my fingers around his hard cock. He groaned. The already impressive muscles in his stomach tightened. I brushed the palm of my other hand across the top of his staff. He moved his arms to grab the rock ledge behind him. He gripped the stone so hard it cracked.

"I don't know how much more I can take," he ground the words out. "It's all I can do not to grab you."

"Patience," I teased. "You know the drill. Good things come to those who wait."

"This—" He shifted his hips. "This is good enough. Let me come."

"Not yet."

I wanted him in my mouth, but that would have to wait.

I rocked against him.

"Julie." He bit down on his lip as he growled my name.

"Jace. Thank you."

"Why are you thanking me right now?" He got the words out slowly, still panting.

"Because I want to. Because you're letting us have this. It means a lot to me that you would share yourself with me." This gorgeous man, who kept to himself, had shared his secret with me when he saved me.

I leaned closer, pressing my breasts against his chest. My clit rubbed against his cock. He threw his head back.

"I'm close," he said.

"I know." I bent forward and touched my lips to his. His lips were minty, like he'd chewed gum recently. He smelled of cedar and woodsmoke. He opened his mouth to meet mine. He pushed his tongue inside my mouth. Unlike the rest of his hot body, his mouth was cool. We kissed, tilting our heads, and I ground against his hardness, over and over. His hands wound through my hair, and now I was close.

But I wasn't done yet.

I pulled back.

He dropped his chin to his chest and breathed.

"I can't wait anymore," he said. He lifted me from the water and placed me on rock ledge. He pushed my legs open and inhaled.

"You smell like lemons. And oranges." He pressed his face between my legs. "I can't get enough." He pushed his finger inside me and his tongue soon joined.

I leaned back on my hands, arching my back. His mouth on me was shattering. I shuddered through my first climax.

"You taste so sweet. So good. But I want the rest of you."

He stood and the rock ledge was the perfect height for me to wrap my legs around his waist.

It was just the right height for him to push his body inside of mine. He held his hard cock at my slick entrance. He rubbed the head across my lips. Back and forth. One hand reached up to squeeze my nipple. My body grew slicker.

"You're so wet. I can't get enough of looking at your tight pussy."

His words sent heated chills down my spine. "I thought you were ready!"

He quirked one eyebrow. "Now who's impatient?

I tried to kick him, but the motion only brought his cock closer to being inside me. "Jace! Please."

"Ready?" he asked.

"Yes. You know I am. I want you inside me."

He groaned and pushed inside, my arousal easing the way. I wrapped my arms around him and buried my face in his neck, inhaling his male scent. I clung to his shoulders while he thrust gently over and over, bringing one hand down to rub between my legs again.

"Harder," I said. I pulled back to fix him with my best stare. "Remember?"

"I don't want to hurt you."

"Don't. Like you said, I survived a plane crash. I stabbed a man. So I can handle you fucking me. I want it." I dug my fingers into his biceps. "Now."

I had never begged a man to fuck me. I liked sex, but I had never craved it like this. I wanted Jace to give me everything he had.

He pulled me tighter to him and thrust again. This time, he wasn't gentle. His thrusts were forceful.

He lifted me off the rock with his strong arms and held me as he drove into me. I threw my head back. "Yes. This. That's perfect." I let my head drop onto his shoulder. Minutes passed, with me in a dreamy haze as I savored the feel of his length. The friction from him hit just the right place inside of me, over and over. Finally, my body pulsed again.

When I cried out, he tensed and began to finish. I could feel him throbbing inside me as he came. "Julie," he moaned. "I need you."

I needed him too. Despite knowing him for one day.

That's crazy, Julie. You've lost it.

I grabbed his shoulders and held on. I didn't care if I was crazy. Now that I had him, I didn't want to let him get away.

After we came down from the intensity of having sex, I lounged in the warm water. Without warning, Jace grabbed me around the waist. He threw me over his shoulder. I yelled as I hung upside down over his powerful body.

He placed his large hand right over my backside. "I like you like this."

Laughing, I wiggled against him as he chuckled. He cupped my bare breast with one hand, while the other rubbed against his skin. He brushed his finger over my nipple. "This is even better."

I kicked my legs. His hands on me sent fiery arousal rushing to the place between my legs, but I needed a rest before round three. "Put me down." I tried to tickle his abs. "I'll get you."

He twisted his abs away from me and captured my wrists easily in one of his big hands. He dropped me carefully onto a soft mattress against the wall. I sprawled across the sheets, letting my legs fall open for him.

Never had I put myself on this kind of display for a man.

With Jace, I liked it.

His eyes grew darker as he surveyed my open legs. "I was wrong. This is the best view." He stood over me, every muscle in his powerful body tight. "I think you'll like this bed better than the safe house cot."

I gave him my sauciest smile. "That depends."

"On what?"

"Will you be in it?"

Jace growled. "I'm going to fuck you in it. I'm going to push my cock into your tight little body." He lowered his body and crawled on top of me, kissing my neck.

His words sent more flames to my already wet clit, and damn, that rumble was sexy. "I'll take that as a yes."

I lifted my body to meet his. "As good as you feel, I can't go again just yet. I'll be ready again in the morning though." I lifted a knee and pressed my thigh against his semi-hard cock.

He pulled me into a hug. "As soon as you're ready, I want you." He smoothed my hair back from my face. "I want to be in you again."

I kissed him on the cheek, relishing the feel of his strong arms around me. "You're certainly more playful now. And talkative."

"My bear feels comfortable."

I basked in that admission. Jace was being real with me. I wanted him even more now.

I shivered.

"Cold?"

"My hair is wet."

He hopped up from the bed and pulled a towel from a crate. "Sit up."

I pushed myself up and he wrapped my hair in the towel with care. It wasn't perfect, but the gesture touched me.

A loud crack shook the cave.

I jumped.

Once I listened, the sound was familiar. "Trees?" I asked.

"Yeah. Branches breaking off."

I pressed my hands to my cold cheeks. "I think the temperature in here dropped."

Jace got up again and gathered every blanket in the cave. He handed me a dry set of clothing. "Let's try to get some rest while we can." He didn't say the words we were both thinking.

Before the Russians show up.

Outside, the storm raged. Howling wind screeched. Tree limbs broke and crashed to the ground. Under the layers of blankets, I shivered. Grateful for his body heat, I snuggled closer to Jace.

Sleep didn't come.

Minutes and hours passed. Still, sleep didn't come.

Dimitri and his men could show up at any time. They'd bust into the cave while we lay defenseless. Jace himself was a weapon, but there were six spies. And they had guns. A lot of them.

I didn't want Jace to think I doubted his strength. I had faith that Jace could defend us, but if the spies got into the cave...

I couldn't foresee a good outcome, even with Jace's superior skills.

I crept from the bed. I found the knife Jace gave me. I preferred to sleep with it in my hand. Those Russian bastards wouldn't let this storm stop them. They were out there, tracking us. Hunting us.

My mind raced. The image of Dimitri blasting Jace with an assault rifle circled in my head, over and over. I had feelings for Jace now. Not a crush. Real feelings. I didn't want him risking his life. Not for me. And not to catch those spies.

I knew what his answer would be. That it was his job. His duty.

Fuck. What was I going to do when this was over?

I shuddered. From the cold. And from the terror of losing this man.

Sensing my distress, Jace wrapped his warm arms around me and pulled me in closer.

JACE

*J*ulie felt good against my body. But she was restless. "Can't sleep?" I asked.

"Just a little achy and cold." She burrowed closer.

"Nightmares?"

"No. Haven't slept long enough for that."

I didn't want to say it, but the nightmares would come soon enough. I expected to have a few myself. I had plenty of material: seeing Julie crash, picking up her unconscious body, and knowing the spies were after her.

I kissed her forehead. "Roll on your side."

Once she settled, I massaged the stiffness from her shoulders. As usual, my body reacted to her. Her proximity aroused me, no matter what kind of insanity was going on around us. I was careful to keep my hips away from her backside. As much as I wanted her, the last thing she needed while she was stressed was to feel my hard cock pressing into her back.

"Bend your neck forward." I kneaded the knots in her

neck. I rubbed circles on her temples. Her muscles relaxed under my touch, but she still squirmed. "Are you hurting?"

"No." She shifted again.

"Tell me what's wrong."

"They could show up at any minute. We won't be ready. We'll be in bed." She raised her hand, showing me the knife she held. She must have gotten up to retrieve it during the night.

"I know we need sleep. But I want to stand at the entrance holding this, while you hold your axe," she said.

There were no platitudes to reassure her. I feared the same. Our choices were shit. We had no phone and no vehicle. The only way to travel was with me in bear form. That meant Julie was unprotected from the storm.

Waiting was all we could do.

I kept rubbing her muscles around her spine. Her worries were legitimate, but after the crash, she needed sleep. Long minutes later, she went boneless. I listened to her breathe. She was asleep.

I stayed awake. No way could I sleep knowing those thugs were after us. Each time I drifted off, I jerked awake to listen.

I would die for Julie. I wouldn't let them take her.

Besides my fear for her life, I had another problem. I wanted to be with her, but would she be with a shifter? It was a big fucking deal. I had allowed her to see my true self.

I wasn't even going to touch the issue of ensuring that she'd keep my secret, not tonight. We'd deal with that later. For now, I needed to know that she'd want me, in spite of all the complications.

I wanted Julie for my own. I wanted to possess her. Even the thought of her going back to her life without me made my blood boil. She would go back to a new plane and to her guy friends.

The thought of her having dinner with those three men

from Fairbanks angered my bear. It was okay for him to insist she never speak to another man, but the human side of me would not fare so well if I tried to control Julie.

My bear felt like she was ours. I wanted the world to know she was mine.

~

One hour of sleep. For the whole fucking night. I rubbed my face. Next to me, Julie scowled.

Even exhausted, her face was gorgeous. In my sweatshirt and pajama pants, her body was luscious. My bear liked her wearing my clothes.

I wanted to strip her. I wanted to crawl on top of her and lose myself in her. She'd said she'd be ready again this morning, for us to make love. My body remembered.

I was hard. My cock was insistent. I'd restrained myself last night, but this was a new day.

I ran my hand over her back. She yanked away. "We need to go."

"Go where?" I tried again. She might need a break from sex. This time I went for a hug.

She crossed her arms. "Jace. This is not the time for that! Quit thinking with your dick!"

Stung, but unwilling to show it, I moved away.

"We need to go to your next safehouse. We're sitting ducks here."

"No. We aren't leaving." She could grumble all she wanted, but she would not be leaving this cave.

"Why?"

"Because the storm is worse." The temps had been well below zero last night. They weren't much higher now.

"How can you even tell? You don't have a radar."

"I can tell. It's instinct."

"You mean like a horse knows when a storm's coming?"

I think she meant that as an insult, but I wasn't going to acknowledge it. "I don't know the mechanics of it, but yes. It's probably a lot like that."

"Well, I don't care what your bear says!"

I motioned toward to cave opening. "Go look for yourself. It's a total whiteout."

"I need to get out of here."

"You're not going anywhere."

"Why do you get to decide? Why is this a unilateral decision?" She flung her arms out. "You didn't even ask how I felt."

"I get to decide because I'm a special forces soldier. I've been trained in how to deal with situations like this, both as a bear and as a human. I've spent hours with the Army, going over what's safe for humans in and out of combat situations."

If I thought that would placate her, then I'd thought wrong.

"You act like I'm a moron. I am a pilot. I've flown through blizzards dozens of times. And I'll fly through dozens more."

Inside, my bear roared at her recklessness. I pushed him back. If we ever did have a relationship, I'd have to find a way to compromise on her bull-headed desire to dive headfirst into danger.

"Right. You are a pilot. But look at what happened the last time you flew."

Low blow, Jace. No pilot in the world could have avoided that sniper's rifle and you know it.

"You asshole." Her eyes flashed. Her mouth twisted. "I crashed because a bunch of Russian gangsters shot my plane."

She was right. I may have crossed the line. But I would not go down the path of debating technicalities with her right now. My goal was keeping her alive.

"Julie, I do not think you are a moron. But I have thought through this. I don't want you in danger. You would not survive out there. It's forty below and there's zero visibility."

I hated that she wanted to take risks. But her impassioned speech appealed, and once again all the blood in my body rushed south. She was furious. I was turned on. I wanted to take her slender body and push her down into the mattress. I wanted to grip her wrists and pin them to the mattress as I thrust into her willing body.

I wanted to show her that I cared about her, and make her understand why she couldn't take risks. "In here, we have a chance."

"No one even knows we're missing. My friends don't. My boss doesn't. No one is coming for us!"

Her words reignited my concern.

Her world was human. Would she keep my secret? Her friends were military; I couldn't let her tell them the truth about me.

What if I angered her enough that she exposed me?

What if her family and friends took exception to the fact that I was a shifter, just like the father who'd burned the wolf shifter alive? What if they didn't stop at just killing me, but wanted to eliminate my entire squadron?

I cared about Julie intensely. In just a short amount of time. But I wasn't sure where her loyalties lay. Mine were with her. I would keep her safe above all else and then I'd do my duty.

As a shifter himself, my CO understood that our shifter nature was an integral part of us. He knew we were some-times compelled to protect our mate above all else.

He'd understand.

Her voice rose. "I am not going to die here! I survived a plane crash yesterday." She smacked her palm against the cave wall. "I am not going to let some two-bit Russian spies take me out."

I agreed, no two-bit spies would be doing anything to her. But I would be the one making sure that didn't happen. Not her.

There was no discussion to be had on this topic. The sooner she learned that, the better. "Are you done?"

She turned her back to me.

I was in control here. Julie did not have to like it. But she would do as I said. I stood over her. "You will not leave. You will stay here until I say we go. If you try to run, I will catch you."

If Julie's glare got any fiercer, I'd go up in flames.

I would not risk her safety, no matter how much she didn't like it. "I know what I'm doing. This is my job. Remember that."

JULIE

"*This is my job. Remember that?*" That's what he had to say to me. What a load of horseshit. Did Jace usually spend this much time with his head up his own ass?

"Fuck you!" I shouted at his retreating back.

That's right, walk away tough guy!

After Jace finished his self-righteous speech, he marched outside and hacked away at a few more trees. As if he needed more firewood. Chop. Chop chop.

Obnoxious tyrant.

Who was he to tell me what to do?

A highly-trained special operations soldier. Who is also a bear part-time.

Shut up, brain. Not helping.

If he was right about staying in the cave and not moving on, and I wasn't convinced that he was, then he could have been a whole lot nicer about it.

He didn't have to sugar-coat it, but he didn't have to act like a barbarian dictator either.

I wasn't going to sit around and pout. I wasn't going to

chop wood, but I could make lunch. I dug through the crate. I found dried meat and a can of vegetable soup.

Copying Jace, I put the soup over the fire in a cast-iron skillet and let it heat.

Listless, I stirred the soup.

Outside, icy pellets pounded the roof of the cave. The wind reached a fever pitch. I didn't have to get up and look outside to know that the world would be completely white and that I wouldn't be able to see my hand two inches in front of my face.

Okay, so he might be right, but he didn't have to be so controlling.

I thought we'd shared something special. The intimacy didn't mean he'd coddle me or give in to what I wanted if it wasn't a smart tactic, but I thought it meant he'd at least hear me out.

Was last night a mistake? My feelings for Jace had grown more intense and maybe—a tiny maybe—I wasn't thinking clearly.

I'd blame it on the head injury.

Had I been irrational?

I had woken up demanding to leave. Neither of us had gotten much sleep the night before. Jace had reached out to me, rubbing his hand over my back, clearly remembering that I'd offered him morning sex.

I hadn't missed the erection that had tented his pants when he'd sat next to me and tried to hug me.

I'd pushed him away.

Rejected him.

That had likely hurt his feelings. It would have crushed mine. If he'd put his hand on my arm and yelled, "now is not the time!" I'd have taken it as a full-on rebuff of me as a person. I'd have concluded that he thought I was an unsexy loser and probably rushed off in a fit of pique.

Being a guy, he wasn't going to tell me he felt rejected. But he'd woken up wanting to be close and I'd stepped all over that idea.

And the icing on the cake was that I'd yelled at him to quit thinking with his dick. As if he hadn't understood what I meant.

I hunched over the soup. Way to go, Julie.

He stomped through the entrance to the cave, dropping bundles of wood into the corner. Wearing just a shirt and pants.

Show-off.

It wasn't fair for him to be so sexy while he was doing anger-chores. His pants clung to the toned muscles of his backside. The muscles in his back strained as he hefted the wood. His biceps flexed as he lay it in piles. His t-shirt stretched across those delicious pecs. Speaking of, I hadn't spent long enough with my mouth on his chest yet.

Yet.

Would he reach for me again?

Would his cock get hard for me?

Would I have another chance to feel his body against mine?

I wanted him inside me again.

I wanted more of him than he might want to give.

I wanted him a whole lot more than I wanted to be right.

Right before the soup boiled, I pulled the pan from the fire and divided it into bowls.

Awkward silence was super fun.

So was not speaking to the guy I wanted most in the world.

I would fix it.

"Lunch is ready," I called out.

Jace froze on his way back outside.

If he walked away from my peace offering, I might just dump this soup on his head.

He propped the axe against the wall.

My stomach wrapped itself into a coiled knot.

He walked over to the blanket by the fire and sat down cross-legged.

The knot in my stomach unwound, just a bit. He might stay pissed, but he was going to eat.

I handed him the soup.

"Thank you," he said.

We sat in silence as we ate.

I swallowed a few times. Why was this so hard? My family would be ashamed of how I'd treated Jace. I hadn't even stopped to acknowledge what he'd done for me.

Deep breath. *Just say it, Julie.* "I never thanked you."

He looked up. "For what?"

"For saving my life."

"Not necessary."

I held up my hand in case he argued. "I know rescue is part of your job. But I do appreciate it. You could have gone straight for the Russians and left me there."

He nodded. "Still not necessary, but you're welcome."

I mimed wiping my forehead. "Whew. If I hadn't done that, I'd have been in for it."

He stared at me with interest. "How so?"

"My family. They don't like to hear about one of their own not respecting others, especially when the other person made a sacrifice for them."

"You'd get a lecture?"

I shook my head. "No lectures. My family, like a lot of traditional Inuits, prefer to use storytelling over just ripping us a new one." I leaned back on my hands. "It could go on for hours."

He laughed.

I sighed in relief. "I have a carved bear in my room." I

nudged him in the ribs. "It's got a fuzzy little face. It's adorable. Looks like you."

He grabbed me and pulled me into his lap. "Not cute. Lethal."

"How about both?" Grateful we hadn't ruined whatever was between us, I relaxed into his lap. "There are a lot of bear stories in Inuit culture; they're highly respected. The bear leader was called Nanook. I've heard stories that, because bears are predators, we imitate the way they hunt." I leaned my head on his shoulder. "I'd heard the Inuit stories about shifters. Do you think my people knew they really existed?"

"I think it's likely. Maybe some were even shifters themselves."

Would I have wanted to be a shifter? I wasn't sure, but the benefits of changing into a bear in the Alaskan frontier were undeniable. "That would come in handy. I was planning to hike the Federal Reserve today. Have you done it before?"

"Yes. As a bear. Not as a person."

"I admit, I'm a little jealous of that." Not having to meticulously pack gear or worry about frostbite were definite perks, as well as being able to navigate the uneven terrain. The physical risks to a bear were not non-existent, but they were greatly reduced.

I stopped myself from suggesting that we hike it together sometime. I wanted more with Jace, but we'd just weathered our first fight. Making plans for the future could wait. "Were you born a shifter?"

"Yeah. It's inherited. I spent most of my time outside as a kid, which was no hardship for a shifter. Grizzly bears are fairly solitary, so we live in groups as humans but we're not as tight as some of the wolf packs."

"Both of your parents are shifters?"

"Yes. My mom was a black bear, but I got the grizzly genes like my dad."

"Was it ever hard? Going to school knowing you were different?" At times, school had been hard enough for me and I was a human. My school had plenty of Inuit students, but the traditions taught in the Anchorage public schools were Western traditions and they didn't always value the native ways.

My cousins assured me attitudes were slowly improving. I hoped so. I wasn't sure I'd send my own future children into an environment that forced them to deny their culture and their ethnicity.

Jace threaded his fingers through my hair. "Some. When I was a teenager, it was hard to cope with having human feelings and bear impulses at the same time. It was hard to date or make friends outside the clan I knew."

I twisted in his arms and hugged him tightly. I breathed in his male scent. Against my leg, I felt his arousal. He was hard. I pointed down. "Um. I thought you'd be mad at me longer than that."

He put his hands on my backside and pulled me tighter. "I wasn't mad. I was frustrated. And I can be frustrated and want you at the same time."

"Frustrated? That's a nice way of saying furious." I grabbed at his sides, tickling him.

"Oh no you don't." He tucked his legs and rolled backward, taking me with him. I tried to scramble away, crawling on all fours. He caught my leg and yanked me back. I laughed so hard I couldn't catch my breath.

He flipped us. He trapped my legs with his. I tried to grab at him, but it was no use. He ducked away, easily evading me until he was on top of me. "Stop tickling me! I'll do whatever you want!"

"Whatever I want?"

"Yes! What do you want? Just tell me." I lifted my body until it was flush against his. He was rock hard.

The feel of his thick arousal inside his cotton pants made my stomach flip, cresting just like I was on a roller coaster. His desire for me sent me reeling. Warm heat rushed between my legs.

I had a pretty good idea what he wanted. And lucky for him, I wanted the same thing.

His voice held a hint of amusement. "I want what all bears want."

"And what's that?"

"Honey."

I threw my head back and laughed. There was that sense of humor again.

I could not get enough of this man.

He positioned me on the blanket, tugging the sweatpants from my body. He shoved my sweatshirt up, baring my breasts. He pushed my legs apart.

I wiggled at the exposure to the cool air.

I stretched out, letting my hair fan around me. My chest heaved.

Jace grinned up at me. He dipped his head down for a taste. "Sweet. Just like I knew you would be."

I reached down to run my fingers through his thick hair. "You had me last night."

"That was a tiny lick. You'd been in the water. Now I really get to taste you." He moaned. "This is the sweetest honey I've ever tasted."

It was a corny line, but I didn't laugh. I was too busy moaning and I refused to think of him doing this with other women. Now that I'd had him, I never wanted him with anyone else.

He closed his mouth over my clit. I wanted to watch, but I couldn't hold my head up. I let it fall back to the blanket.

One of his fingers pushed into me. "I could do this forever," he said.

My back arched. I writhed, unable to stay still. My laughter faded, replaced by pure lust. He mastered my body like no one else could.

Jace grabbed my ankles and placed my feet back on the blanket. He placed one strong palm over my hip bone. "Don't move."

I moaned at the command in his voice. His raw power sent a shiver through my veins. I wanted to do whatever he said.

I wanted him turned on, ready for me, always.

Just as I was turned on for him.

His mouth went back to my clit and I grabbed my breasts myself and squeezed my nipples.

"I like seeing that." He raised up briefly and peered at me. "Leave your hands there."

I thrashed, moaning. He put one hand back on my hip, pressing me into the blanket. A second finger joined the first. His tongue flicked over my clit, over and over.

All that raw power in this man and he could harness it into pleasuring the most delicate part of my body.

I'd never experienced ecstasy like this. Jace was the reason.

Delicious pressure built inside me. "Jace."

"Next time I'm going to have you put your own fingers down here while I watch."

I bucked against his hand that still pressed me down. "I want to see that," he said. "You, touching yourself, giving yourself pleasure." He sucked on my clit. "Would you do it for me? Would you pleasure yourself while I watch?"

"Yes! Jace!"

"Say it."

"I'll touch myself. You'll watch."

Heaven help me, I'd never wanted anything like that. I'd never wanted to put myself on exhibit like that. I was more turned on now than I'd ever been in my life. Flames ate me up from the inside and fueled the fire in my core.

"You're going to come for me," he said. "I want to see it. I want to feel it."

He pushed his fingers up and curled them. Heat exploded inside my body. "Your body is gripping me."

My orgasm pulsated through me. I felt every wave against his fingers.

"You're not done."

"I can't." My hands fell to my sides. My head lolled.

"You will. For me." His mouth lowered to my breast. He sucked and nipped, then replaced his mouth with his hand. He squeezed my nipples, first one, then the other. He knelt back between my legs and rubbed the head of his cock over my clit.

"Jace! Please. Inside me."

"Not yet." He grabbed my hands and put them back on my breasts.

He moved back between my legs, putting his mouth on me again. He moved faster this time, pulling my lips apart with one hand while pushing his fingers into my body.

"You're so wet. Your body wants this."

I cried out. "Don't stop!"

"You make me crazy. I've never wanted anyone this much." His tongue joined his finger inside me and I came again, wave after wave crashing over my body until I sagged, limp from pleasure.

He scooped me up, cradling me in his arms. "Julie." He sealed his mouth to mine. "I don't have words for how amazing you are. That was incredible."

I gave him a lazy smile. "Jace."

He grabbed a clean blanket and pulled it over us.

"Give me a minute," I said.

"There's nothing you need to do."

I reached my hand down between his legs. His cock was hard. It grew harder in my hand. I liked seeing the evidence of how much he wanted me. His persistent state of arousal flattered me. "You didn't get to finish," I said.

He rubbed his thumb across my cheek. "I want to do that with you."

I cuddled into him. "I'm glad. I want to do the same." I yawned. "After a nap." I drifted off thinking about how well I'd do returning the favor.

I stretched my arms above my head. Outside, the storm raged on. Inside the cave, the hot springs bubbled and the fire warmed us. Behind me, Jace's erection pressed into my back.

I backed my ass up against him. "Someone's awake."

He pushed my hair aside and kissed the back of my neck. "When I'm with you, that's a permanent condition."

I spun in his arms. "Now I'm ready."

Jace groaned. "I won't argue this time."

I pushed myself into a sitting position. "I want you in my mouth."

He shuddered. "God, Julie. I don't know if I can handle that."

"I know you've had someone go down on you before."

"Yes. But they weren't you. And no one's ever said it like that. Hearing you say the words—" He dipped his head and exhaled. "It does something to me." He stood up. He grabbed an extra blanket and folded it in half in front of him. He rubbed his hand over my cheek. "On your knees."

I knelt. Being on my knees for him felt good. It felt right.

I'd never let anyone on this planet tell me what to do. But with Jace...

It was hot. I wanted more. I'd let him hold me down. I'd let him fuck me, over and over and over until neither of us could take it anymore.

He held my head steady. He pushed his thick cock into my mouth. I ran my lips over the head. I made a humming sound until he groaned.

He pulled back. "Jesus, Julie. You feel so good." He pushed forward. I hollowed my cheeks and sucked. I'd read that hint online, many years ago, in one of those ridiculous *Ten Ways to Keep Your Man* articles. He panted. "Stop."

I pulled back. My lips tingled from his size.

"Stay still. I'm going to fuck your mouth."

I gripped his thighs while he took control. He cradled my jaw and my nipples tightened.

My pussy was so wet I dripped onto the blanket. I squeezed my legs together, desperate for friction.

I moaned and hummed as he fucked my mouth with his big cock. I zoned out, satisfied with giving him pleasure. After several minutes, he pulled away with a gasp. He joined me on the blanket. "I need to be in you."

"You can have me." I lay back. He followed me down, wrapping one arm under my shoulders. His other hand found its way between my legs.

"Your pussy is so wet." He ran his fingers across my damp thighs. He nudged me. "Flip over to your stomach. Hands and knees."

Once I was in position, he put a hand on my lower back. He pushed his cock into me. He plunged in, all the way. His body pressed tight against my backside.

He nuzzled my neck. He kissed my jaw. He whispered into my ear. "I can't get enough of you." He leaned back to rub his hands over my ass. "I could look at you like this all day."

"Then do it." I fell to my elbows, breathing hard. I pressed my ass back against him, grinding.

"You don't know—" His cock slammed into me. "What you're offering."

"I can take it."

He rammed his cock in, faster but with care. He thrust for several long minutes. "Jesus, Julie. I'm on the brink." He bent over me and nosed at my neck. He pulled out.

I collapsed, my body flat against the bed.

"You have no idea how much I want you." He lifted me and turned me back over. "I need to see your face."

His lips met mine as he kissed me. His tongue pressed into my mouth. My core ached with need, desperate to be filled up again. Never had a man possessed me like this.

He leaned up on his elbows. "This is mine." He rubbed his fingers over my clit.

Yes. My body belonged to him. I wanted my heart to belong to him too.

"Please."

"Please what?"

"Don't tease. Fuck me."

I writhed against the sheet.

He rubbed the head of his cock over my opening. "I love how wet you get for me."

"It's because I want you so much." That was the truth.

Sex had never been like this. Not even close. Each moment with Jace was better than the last.

He pushed into me again. This time he lay with me, face to face. He rolled us on our sides and kissed me. His thrusts slowed and became gentle. He peppered kisses on my cheeks, my forehead, my nose, and even my chin.

I held tight to his shoulders. If I closed my eyes, I could

pretend that we weren't trapped in a cave, chased by terrorist spies. We could be on vacation. A ski trip to the Swiss Alps.

No. Somewhere tropical. I let my mind drift as he rocked into my body. "I took a job last year where I flew from St. Thomas to St. John. U.S. Virgin Islands."

He rolled his hips, hitting the best spot inside my body. "Yeah?"

"Yeah. We should go," I mumbled, lost in a floaty haze. "Cruz Bay. Beach. Sand. Margaritas. Opposite of here."

Jace rested his forehead against mine. "Sounds perfect."

My eyes flew open. I'd just suggested we go on vacation together. We hadn't even discussed what we'd do once we'd eliminated the spies.

Jace hadn't freaked out. He'd rolled with it.

I wasn't going to push it. This was the same man who'd avoided me like the plague before I crashed his plane. But now I knew who he was, all the secret parts of him.

There was something about being on the run together in a life-threatening situation that brought people together.

Not to mention that Jace trusted me with the big reveal: his life as a shifter, a secret he guarded closely. It was a secret I would take to the grave.

I pressed my knees into his sides as he sped up.

"I'm almost there. Being inside you, it's perfect," he said.

His cock grew harder as he came inside me. He rolled onto his back, taking me with him. He murmured a few words as we lay there, still joined together. I don't think I was supposed to hear them. But I'm pretty sure he whispered, "you're the best thing that's ever happened to me."

I felt sorry for all those women who'd come before me. If they'd really seen him, they'd have never wanted to let him go. So many of them had only gotten tiny pieces of him.

But not me. I got every part of him.

JACE

We woke up tangled together. For breakfast, we dug through the food crate and picked out several cans of fruit and some packaged pepperoni.

"I could get used to this," Julie said.

So could I.

I wanted more time with her.

Time without the looming threat. Without the constant fear for her life. I draped a blanket over her shoulders and we sat by the fire, eating soggy fruit from a bowl.

My body was worn out in a pleasant way from all the love-making Julie and I had done. I'd thought of our intimacy as making love yesterday, but the concept had been vague to me, even one day ago. Since then we'd had a massive fight, made up, and slept together again.

Julie had given herself over to me in ways I hadn't imagined. We'd taken turns giving each other pleasure. I'd have been thrilled to put her pleasure first, but she'd insisted that we take turns.

I hadn't expected her to let me take charge in bed. But she had. And she'd seemed to enjoy it and relish getting off on it.

Making love to her face-to-face was my favorite, but fucking her mouth and then fucking her from behind had gotten me off hard.

My body had been on high alert ever since. I couldn't wait to do it again.

Even while stoking the fire or brushing my teeth, I was in a constant state of arousal with a rock hard cock.

I pressed a cherry to Julie's lips.

She took the cherry in between her teeth but nipped at my fingers first. She bit down, grinning at me.

I groaned at the feel of her lips on my fingers. "I need some grapes and I could serve you like you're Cleopatra."

"You can spoil me all you want once we—"

A deafening crack echoed through the cave.

Julie jumped.

I sprung to my feet.

That was no tree.

Another loud crack boomed. This time dust fell from the cave wall. I threw myself on top of Julie. "Stay down," I hissed. If I could get her under the bed, she'd have some cover. "Once I get you hidden, stay there."

She dug her fingernails into my arm. "You can't go out there! They're shooting at us!

Another shot rang out. This one was much closer.

She was right. If they were walking into the cave, then I couldn't confront them in my human form. They'd kill me first.

Then they'd kill Julie.

I would never let that happen.

I didn't keep guns in the cave. When I fought, I fought as a bear.

Julie had her knife. I vowed to get her a gun after this ended.

Dimitri and his crew didn't know I was a shifter. I'd have to count on the element of surprise.

A shadow appeared at the edge of the cave. "My fair Julie. We meet again." It was a man's voice with a Russian accent.

The head spy.

Hearing him say her name spiked my blood pressure. My bear clawed at me, desperate to get out. If Julie were safe, I'd charge against him now, regardless of the consequences.

I signalled to Julie to keep quiet, but I should have known how well that would work.

"Dimitri, you asshole!" She lifted her head from where I was trying to keep her flat against the ground. "If you don't want to die a grisly death, you should leave. Now."

"It appears as though we have interrupted your, how do you say, *love nest*. Just as you have interrupted the job I have planned to do." He made a tsking sound. "I bet you are beautiful when naked, Julie. This bear has taken your body for his own, no?"

My chest heaved. Sharp bear canines shot from my human mouth. How dare this swine mention my Julie in that way.

No. I wasn't ready to transform yet.

Kill him.

My bear was right. But I had to stay human. For now.

I looked at Julie to gauge her reaction. Far from being paralyzed with fear, she made a gagging motion with her hand. "I'm gonna puke," she whispered.

Dimitri was still prattling. "There is a break in the storm. Most fortuitous for us. You would agree, yes?"

Was he serious right now? This moron sounded like a cartoon character.

"You did me a favor, Julie Teslo. You showed Ivan to be a sniveling coward. He will serve his country one last time.

Then he will die with you both." The moron made a clapping sound. "Ivan, Sergei, Vladislav, come. Viktor and Tomas, stand guard. Let us end this hunt."

The shadowy figure took shape as Dimitri stepped farther into the cave. He was a little guy, not even close to six feet tall.

My bear wasn't going to tolerate my being a human much longer. He pushed at me, scratching at me to let him out. He was on the verge of shifting whether I liked it or not.

I'd trained for this. I'd carried out countless missions. This was the first time I'd ever had a personal connection to my targets.

Fighting inside a cave was not a great strategy. Our best bet would be getting out. Me as a bear, with Julie on my back.

My feelings for Julie tugged at me. I'd fought six men before, but never while carrying a human.

"Julie." Dimitri's sing-song voice grated. "I believe we will spend quality time together before you die."

My chest rumbled. The urge to tear his throat out gnawed at me. I heard Julie's pulse speed up. Her heart raced. I wanted to reassure her.

I pressed my mouth right up to Julie's ear. "I'm going to shift. You're going to have to get on my back and hold on. You can't stay in here. They'd pick us off, one by one."

She lifted her chin. "I'm ready when you are."

For all his bluster, Dimitri was a dumb piece of shit. He and the other five goons strolled up in a group. Three of them faced us, the other two faced the woods.

This was our chance.

"Stay as flat as you can. We'll only have a few seconds before they start firing again." I could not lose her. "Keep your head down."

Her eyes blazed. "Let's do this."

I would never stop being impressed by her bold courage.

With an ear-splitting roar, I shifted from human to bear. Julie didn't hesitate. She jumped on my back. She gripped my fur.

I charged.

One of the rats screamed, *"Ty che, blyad!"*

Julie snorted. "I've heard Dimitri say that before. I'm pretty sure it means *what the fuck?"*

I pushed my body into the men. The first two hit the ground in a messy heap.

Dammit. Dimitri had dodged me. Faced with a pissed off grizzly bear, the coward ducked behind a tree.

Julie's hands tightened in my fur. "Piss off, you dumb fuckers!"

The two outside, Viktor and Tomas, who'd been told to stand guard, tried to run too. I knocked one aside. The other flailed. He stayed up until Julie kicked her foot out. She nailed him right in the head.

Only Dimitri was left standing, but he had to go. He'd dropped his gun when I charged, but now he fumbled, trying to grab it from the snow.

I raced forward. I slammed into Dimitri. He flew backward and his head hit a tree. He slumped sideways into the snow.

I wouldn't be lucky enough for him to be dead. He'd wake up and come after us soon enough. Ideally, I'd stop and kill them all, or at least secure them. But with six, there was no way to do that without risking Julie.

The first two I'd pushed aside were already beginning to stir.

I had to get Julie somewhere safe.

I ran into the blizzard. I didn't look back.

Julie's legs tightened across my back. "You did it, Jace. They're all down."

The coat I'd given Julie was in the cave. She wore a sweatshirt, sweatpants and thick socks. That was it. If I didn't get her inside soon, she'd freeze to death.

91

It was so freaking cold that every part of my body went numb. It had been awhile since I had any feeling in my arms and legs. Jace had been at it for an hour at least, running as fast as he could.

He was able to dodge trees with ease and when we hit streams or creeks, he just plowed right through.

Very impressive stamina. But hey, I'd already experienced his stamina first-hand.

I smirked into his fur. Did it count if no one could see it?

If I fell asleep, would I roll off into the snow? What then? My head drooped to one side.

I pictured my fantasy Caribbean vacation with Jace. He'd seemed up for it last night. I'd never been to Grand Cayman. After a romantic flight, we'd rent a cabana on the beach and sink our toes into the sand. I looked forward to sipping margaritas while the sun beat down on us.

I imagined inside our cabana on an already secluded beach. The sun would set, casting an amber glow over the sea. I'd spread my legs so Jace could see how wet I was for him. How ready.

He'd make me hold onto the legs of the chaise lounge while he pushed my knees farther apart. He'd pull his swollen staff from his swim trunks and rub it over my heaving breasts. Then he'd rub it over my stomach, trailing his way slowly down to my wet cave. I couldn't help a small giggle; I couldn't stop with the bear jokes even when I wasn't trying.

The wetter I got, the more he'd rub until I begged him to fill me up for the first time.

The second time, immediately after, would be in the ocean while warm ocean waves crested over our bodies.

Mmmm.

I really needed to tell him about this fantasy.

I think he'd like it. "Hey, Jace…we should get a towel. You can wear a—"

I slipped sideways.

At least I'd die now, loopy from a nice beach fantasy with Jace, instead of with Dimitri and his goons.

I fell.

For a second, I was weightless. The snow would be cold, but it would kill me quickly.

Goodbye, Jace. I know it's fast, but I think I love you.

Love?

Did I love Jace? I was pretty sure that I did.

I blinked.

Instead of lying face-down in the icy snow, I was being shaken by an irate Jace. A very human Jace. "Julie. You cannot sleep. I know this is terrible. But you have to stay awake."

My face went to a scowl. "Did you slap me?"

Regret clouded Jace's handsome face. "I didn't know what else to do."

My frown turned into a grin. "Don't feel sad. It worked. Hey. Are you naked? That's nice." I tried to touch his well-developed pecs but my hand didn't cooperate.

"Julie," he barked. "Pay attention."

"What?"

Why was Jace cross? He was really nice looking. He should be happy about that and also about our future trip to the beach. I wanted to touch him. But I couldn't make my arms work. Speaking of my hands, Jace had somehow tucked them under his arms. "I'm going to get you warmed up. Then we need to start running again."

Too soon, pins and needles prickled through my skin. "We can go now. I feel a little bit better."

"Just a little while longer," he promised. "Then you can rest."

He shifted back and I clung to him while he ran.

I hung on for another fifteen minutes or so until my hands were numb again. I let my eyes close.

Before I knew what was happening, Jace was human again. He flung me over his shoulder and ran into a small log cabin. I dangled upside down. Blood rushed to my head.

I couldn't find the words to ask what we were doing.

JACE

For the second time in two days, Julie was unconscious. The first time, I'd been alarmed. I'd worried about her, more than I would for most people. This time, all I felt was terror.

Julie had been out of her mind. She'd rambled about a chaise lounge, of all things. Most of her words had been incoherent. It had scared the shit out of me.

If this was what having a mate was like, how did any shifter survive it?

I'd relaxed just a fraction when she'd told me she could hold on and then she'd successfully gripped my fur for the last few miles to the cabin.

Now she was out cold.

I'd never expected to have a mate. I'd grown up close with the females in my clan and they felt more like sisters to me. We were encouraged to branch out to find mates in other clans, but it felt too forced to me.

My mother tried to set me up with shifters who lived in other states, but a blind date seemed tedious and false. My bear didn't want to either.

Even if I'd wanted to leave Alaska, which I definitely didn't, I didn't have time to date. I was generally away from home, running missions with my team.

Very rarely, when one of us was given permission by clan elders to date a human, most of the clan disapproved. They knew it was sometimes necessary because there were so few of us.

They generally kept their comments to themselves out of respect, but sometimes the shifter would feel the thin layer of disquiet when the human mate was around.

I understood the hesitancy after hearing about the tragedy that befell my wolf brother who was burned alive. But I would not want to introduce Julie to a family life where she'd be a constant suspect.

My father said his sister had married a human man. But they lived in London and we'd never met him.

What would my parents say if I told them I'd found a mate?

A human mate.

I couldn't believe I was now considering Julie a mate. Me, the human part, not just my bear.

Would the elders intervene?

Would my commanding officer?

I was getting ahead of myself. Just because I wanted Julie didn't mean she wanted me. I was convenient right now. I'd saved her. She had no other options.

I believed that she cared about me.

But to commit herself to a shifter who was a full-time soldier? It was a lot to ask.

At least she'd understand the strong family ties.

Her Inuit relatives sounded like they functioned a lot like a bear clan.

I laid her on the bed.

Before I could get her warmed up, I checked the perimeter. I didn't think Dimitri and his thugs could have tracked us here, but I wasn't taking chances.

I found nothing suspicious.

Back inside, I set to work getting the space heater on. I was immensely grateful that this safehouse had propane and running water.

Once I had some heat running, I covered Julie with every blanket in the cabin. I got a fire going. I laid down with her, tucking her hands and feet against my skin. I rested my forehead against her shoulder. Her pulse beat with a steady rhythm. She would live. Thankful for that, I prayed she'd make it through this without frostbite.

Hours later, Julie stirred.

"Jace?"

"I'm here."

"Want to go to the beach? Do you surf?"

My blood froze. Was Julie worse off than I'd expected? Was she hallucinating? Her words had been slightly slurred and her eyes were still closed.

"We're in Alaska." I put my hands on her cheeks. They were still chilly. "We're in one of my safehouses."

She took my hand in hers. "I know. Just planning our vacation."

I let my shoulders slump.

I'd had no choice but to run with her. She'd had no protection from the blizzard, just a layer of cotton. I knew how to treat hypothermia in humans; it was part of my training.

"No beach?" she asked.

"I would love to go to the beach with you." I promised myself that even if we didn't end up together, we'd take a trip to the beach.

She snuggled into me.

"And surf?"

I'd surfed every day when I'd been stationed in California. My bear liked the warm waters of the Pacific just as well as he liked the frigid sea in Alaska. "Yes. We can race."

"Don't wanna move there. Just visit." She patted my chest. "Alaska is home."

"Alaska is home for me too."

She tried to move her hand to pat my cheek but missed. "You from here?"

"Yeah. I was born in Naknek. It's a tiny town near Katmai National Park and Preserve. Makes it easy for us to shift and hunt in our bear forms." My clan was still there.

I was relieved to see her bright smile. "You never talk about your family."

I shrugged. "Habit. It was trained out of us. Less risk when no one knows we have one."

The smile dropped from her face. "I won't say anything. I promise."

I'd have to broach the subject again when she was less woozy. But even now, I valued her promise to keep my secret.

I lay with her. I inhaled her scent. Afraid to leave her, I watched her sleep. Finally, about an hour later she curled onto her side. She opened her eyes. They were sharp again, with focus. Julie was back.

My bear was just as relieved as I was.

"Were you watching me sleep?"

"I was."

She poked me in the ribs. "Creeper."

I ignored her attempt at making light of how scared she had to be. I could see the wariness in her eyes. I saw nerves that weren't there this morning before Dimitri found us.

"How do you feel?"

"Fine."

Sure, her flat voice with zero inflection really reassured me that she was fine.

Attacked by spies, shot at, became hypothermic. All in a day's work.

I was freaking out. I'd never been hypothermic, but I'd been attacked by spies and shot at plenty of times. The first time it happened, I had not been calm, cool and collected.

I'd never tell a soul, but after a mission gone bad in Canada, I'd had an epic meltdown once I was alone in the showers.

"Jace seriously. Stop fretting. I'm good." She pursed her lips. "Do you think we really have a chance of escaping from Dimitri? How long can this cat and mouse game go on?"

"Yes. We have a chance. A great one. In that scenario, we are not the mouse. We are the cat."

I believed that. I would not give up. Julie lay back down beside me and settled against me. While she slept, I plotted how we'd handle Dimitri.

I'd go out to face him—and each one of his men—head on. Tactically, that was our best shot. I was done putting Julie at risk.

JULIE

When I woke up, my arms and legs were stiff, but I was alive. And warm. Outside, the gray sky was visible. The lack of howling wind was noticeable.

A fire blazed in a brick fireplace. I had never appreciated a fire more.

I found Jace at the kitchen table with a whetstone in one hand and a wicked-looking hunting knife in the other. A large collection of knives lay in rows across the table.

I put my hands on his shoulders. "This looks ominous. I thought you'd sharpen your claws instead of knives."

Jace didn't laugh at my clear wit. I rubbed my head. It was possible that I was still sluggish from my hypothermic nap.

"See if you like this one." Jace handed me a knife.

He was all business. I guessed facing a battle would do that to a soldier.

"You said you threw a knife at one of the Russians. And it stuck in his arm."

I turned the blade over in my hand. It was a good fit. "Yeah. Ivan." I pointed to the soft place between the top of my humerus bone and my collarbone. "It wedged right there."

"Apparently it did enough damage that Dimitri felt the need to mention it." He put one blade aside and picked up the next.

"Yeah, Dimitri basically called him a weenie in front of all of us." I surveyed the knives. "I'd feel bad, but you know. Terrorists."

Jace's face hardened. "I want you to have options."

I laid my hand on Jace's arm. "What are you thinking?"

Jace dropped the whetstone and the knife and turned to face me. "I'm done with them chasing us. I'm going out to meet them. Face to face, one by one."

"I want to help you." In a split second, I saw the big giant *no* written all over his face. "Listen, I caught them. They were opening the mail I carry. Bringing weapons into our country." I wanted to see them pay just as much as anyone. "They trashed my plane."

Jace's jaw tightened.

I could tell where this was headed. "You want me to stay here."

"Yes."

I was the one who'd walked in on Dimitri and set off this wild chase. I wanted to be out there. However, I could be honest with myself — I was not a soldier; I wasn't trained to fight. My strength was flying, and I was good with outdoor survival too.

I was a pretty good shot, but I didn't have a gun. I hated it, but he had a point. I was desperate to go but catching the spies was Jace's job.

It would be easier on Jace if I stayed here. "I don't like it. But I will."

He embraced me. "I can't focus on them if I'm worried about you. We've already had too many close calls. I need you safe."

JACE

Never had I anticipated my need for another person to be this all-consuming. Julie's life had been at risk almost non-stop in the last twenty-four hours. Each of those times, we'd been pursued, unable to stop and plan. Now that we had a break in the storm, I refused to waste it.

I was going after the Russians.

I admired the hell out of her, wanting to go after them too. I loathed leaving her here unprotected. She'd have the knives. In the future, I was going to hide a few guns in my safehouses. Along with a few satellite phones.

I breathed in. The future. I wanted Julie in my future. I wanted her in my life. It wouldn't seem like it to most humans, but telling her where I was born was a monumental admission for me. For any shifter.

I'd underplayed how rigid our clans were about keeping our information to ourselves. Even my brothers in arms, all shifters themselves, didn't know where I was from.

But Julie did.

I pulled her toward me, into my lap. As usual, when she was close, I was hard. I never stopped wanting her.

She wiggled her bottom against my arousal. "Someone's happy to see me."

"Always." I spun her so she was facing me, straddling my lap. I tucked my hand into her sweatpants. I brushed my finger against her mound. "No panties."

She bucked against me. "Didn't have any."

I growled at the memory of her being forced to flee without proper gear. I pushed it aside. She wasn't upset. I would manage my fury.

I pushed a finger inside her, satisfied to find her wet. "Once this is done, I'll take you out, properly. We'll go to a nice steakhouse." I added a second finger. "You won't wear panties under your clothes then either."

"Yes." She writhed, pushing herself deeper onto my fingers. "I never wear dresses. But that night, I'll wear a dress. I have a black one. Fitted waist, v-neckline, flared skirt. I'll be bare underneath."

I couldn't stop my groan. My cock throbbed harder. "You'll sit next to me in a booth. While I order for us, you'll know I can dip my fingers inside you, just like this."

Julie put her hands on my shoulders and lifted herself, up and down, riding my fingers. "Don't stop," she moaned, nearly breathless. "I'll cross my legs at first. Then I'll spread them open, just a bit. Right while the waiter is there."

"He will not be allowed to see."

"No. Just you."

I would get as kinky as Julie was willing to go, but I'd have to draw the line at exhibitionism. She'd responded so well to my instructions so far and even liked the restaurant scenario. I looked forward to finding out what else she might want.

I flicked my thumb over her clit. Her head fell back. Her

long black hair swung as she climaxed. I kissed her neck. "That's one."

She folded her body against mine. "Push your pants down."

Hastily, I complied.

I looked down, my erection rigid, yearning away from my body, trying to find it's way to her.

I took Julie by the hips and lifted her into the air. She gripped my shoulders; her fingernails dug into my skin. I positioned her right above my cock. She moaned as the head of my manliness grazed the lips of her vagina. I met her lips with a fierce kiss. "You are so beautiful. Sometimes I can't believe it."

I pulled her down hard. The motion pushed my cock deep into her as she moaned with approval.

"Jace," she cried out as I filled her in one motion.

I ripped her sweatshirt off. She arched and I took her breast into my mouth. I circled her nipple with my tongue. "Julie." I moved to the other breast as her body surged against mine. I wanted her. Now and after this was over. Would she want the same thing?

I'd have to convince her.

I would not let her slip away from me.

I wrapped my arms around her. I gripped her ass and lifted her, again and again.

"You feel so good."

She circled her hips. Her breasts bounced in front of my face. Her inner walls rippled against my cock, in wave after wave. I roared as my climax coursed through me.

Julie and I slouched against each other. "I don't want you to go," she whispered.

"I don't want to leave you either." I tightened my arms around her. "But I have to deal with them. Even if it wasn't my duty, I wouldn't rest until they were dead. They're not just a threat to our country. They're a threat to you too."

Her lips were warm against my neck. "I know."

I gathered her up and carried her to the tiny free-standing tub. It wasn't fancy. But I had running water here. I let the water heat up while we brushed our teeth, then I folded us both into the bath. I only had bar soap, but I lathered my hands and washed her hair, pulling her silky mane to the side and kissed the nape of her neck.

She hummed, grinning at me over her shoulder. "My turn," she said.

She rubbed the soap into foam and ran it through my hair. I let my head fall forward. Her hands tingled on my scalp. I loved being with her this way.

Was I in love?

I had never used that word. What I felt for her seemed like more than love. My desire for her was primitive. It consumed me.

"You look serious," she said. "Are you worried?"

"I'm worried about you. If I knew you'd be safe, I'd feel a lot better."

"I'll hide if I need to," she said. "And I have the knives. Sometime soon I'll show you how good I am at throwing them."

I would enjoy watching her aim knives at a target, once she was no longer in danger. After we rinsed the soap from our bodies, I kissed her nose.

I grabbed two towels. I wrapped one around my waist and I began to dry her skin. Even fully sated, I enjoyed rubbing a towel over her naked body. I did have it bad.

The mood shifted from teasing to heavy as she pulled on her clothes in silence.

I love you.

I practiced saying it in my head.

My bear approved.

I let the towel drop from my waist. I hung it over a chair. I had to give her one last kiss. I pressed my mouth against hers, tasting the cool mint from our shared toothpaste.

With the taste of her still on my tongue, I shifted.

My bear was ready. He wanted his mate safe.

In bear form, I tore through the woods. Without the blustery wind and thick snow, my bear was attuned to tracking the spies. An hour into my sprint, I found them.

They travelled together in a Jeep. I followed them, keeping pace with the vehicle easily. After seeing where they were headed, I raced ahead. I found a small clearing with a boulder nearby. I hid. I waited.

They trundled along, unsuspecting. Idiots. All six, traveling in the same Jeep. I leapt from behind the tree.

I brought five hundred pounds of enraged grizzly bear to rest in front of them.

This far out, no one clears the road. There are no snow plows. No snow blowers. In several feet of snow, the Jeep brakes screeched. The Russians fishtailed and skidded on the snowy road, coming to rest in a snowbank.

I shoved at the Jeep with my shoulder. They would not be driving away from this.

The cowards squealed as I rocked the Jeep sideways with my shoulder. I used my sheer mass to get it up on two wheels and gravity did the rest.

The spies scrambled, struggling to keep their guns as they tumbled like rocks inside the Jeep.

I busted through the side window with my paw. I plucked the first spy out with my teeth. This one was called Tomas. With an earth-shattering howl, I flung him to the ground.

I gave his body a sharp twist. I tugged until I heard his neck break.

I left his body to cool on the ground.

I caught the next one on his belly, crawling from the Jeep. This one was the spy Dimitri had called Viktor. I sank my teeth into his jugular vein. Blood spurted. I dropped him to lie beside the first.

The other three were gone. I'd been too slow. I crept forward, sniffing. There. I followed the scent until I found him in a ditch, flattened to the ground.

He muttered to himself in Russian. I wondered if this was the one Julie stabbed. Ivan. I didn't have time to check. I flipped him over and stabbed my claws into his heart. His death was quick, which was too good for any of them. If Julie had woken up in her plane, without me there, there was no guarantee that her death would have been as easy any of theirs.

Two more to go.

My boss would want me to leave one of them alive for questioning. To find out what other heinous plans they'd hatched to unleash on an unsuspecting outpost but he was going to have to deal with disappointment.

From the moment they'd shot at Julie, they'd written their own death sentences. What my boss wanted wasn't a factor. Only Julie's safety mattered.

I paced, scenting the air. They couldn't have gone far on foot.

Pain exploded in my shoulder.

I rocked backward. That was a bullet.

I'd been shot. I dropped to a lower crouch and panted. Blood seeped from my left shoulder. One of the men had shot me. It was a high-calibre weapon. Nausea rolled through my body. My stomach rebelled. I gagged.

I dragged myself to the Jeep for cover. I stuck my face in

the snow and gave myself a minute to regroup. I couldn't stop now.

I scanned the tree line.

Within minutes, one of the branches rustled but I couldn't make out a human form.

Damn it. That meant there were two left. Another plus Dimitri.

The lead motherfucker who'd threatened Julie. He wasn't much of a mastermind, but he was rotten to the core.

I wished I could call out his name. Minutes passed. I caught flashes of movement, of sound, of scent. But I didn't find either one.

Too late, I realized they must have escaped early on, if they were even together.

I knew at least one of them would be headed straight toward Julie.

I ran. The barbed pain in my shoulder took a backseat. I had to protect my mate.

JULIE

I paced for the rest of the day and night. Yes, Jace was capable. But he was taking on six unrepentant spies by himself. I hated waiting.

I had no appetite, but I forced myself to open a pack of beef jerky. I wanted to be ready if Jace came back and we went on the run again.

I found a piece of lumber to practice my knife throwing. I set it up against the wall, but I never got around to practicing on how to throw the knife.

The front door crashed open, bringing a burst of frigid air inside.

I spun. "Jace! Are you—"

I froze. It wasn't Jace. It was Dimitri. He tugged his hat and goggles off and let them drop to the floor.

Before he could raise his gun, I flung my knife. It grazed Dimitri's cheek. It cut into his skin, but he didn't scream. A slow smile curved over his face. Dammit! I hadn't gotten used to the knife Jace had given me yet and now I'd missed when it counted most.

He pulled his glove off and wiped the blood from his cheek. "My dear Julie, that does sting."

"I am not your dear anything. Don't say my name."

He pointed a revolver at me. "From where I stand, you're not in a position to make demands. So, I will say your name, *krasivyy tsveto.*" He ran his nasty finger down my arm. "It means beautiful flower."

He twisted his thin lips into a crude imitation of a smile. "And you will say my name many, many times before this night is over." He bent to pick up my knife. "It's a shame that your bear hero can't be here to watch what I do with you."

I swallowed. I didn't know much about spies outside action movies and novels, so I'd have to go with that. "So what's going to happen to you when your boss finds out you botched your job and got owned by one soldier and a woman with a knife?"

"*Zatknis!* You do not know what you speak about."

I needed to keep him talking, right? That part had to be true. "So tell me."

He took slow, stalking steps toward me, shedding outdoor gear as he approached. "I will be lauded when I succeed with this mission. Collateral damage is a part of any mission."

Collateral damage? Did that mean the others were dead?

"Where are the rest? Ivan and the others?"

"They are hunting your Jace. I shall quite enjoy having him as a trophy. A bearskin rug will be the right addition to my collection, yes?"

Oh god. *Jace.* My stomach churned. I had to take a few quick breaths to keep from vomiting all over the floor.

Those words, that image, would never leave me.

He's just trying to get you off balance. Pull it together.

I didn't want Dimitri to see how much he'd rattled me. "You won't catch him."

"Ah. That is where you are wrong. I don't need to catch him. Jace and his beast will not let his lady suffer. How would you say it? I believe he will be your knight in shining armor."

He was right. Jace wouldn't leave any human to suffer at Dimitri's hands. I wasn't sure if I was his lady or not, but he would fly in here, full speed ahead if he thought he could save me, regardless of the consequences to himself.

"So I'm your bait."

"I prefer to think of you as my prize, yes?"

This guy could really not be any more of a cliché villain. He even had a goatee.

"I will share a secret with you. The history channel is really quite a bore." He moved the gun to his left hand and picked up a knife. "I have quite the distaste for the American habit of television consumption." He sneered. "Ivan has developed a fascination for it. I do fear that if we had been stationed in Los Angeles that he would have defected." He chuckled. "I am merely joking. Despite his incompetence, Ivan is loyal to our homeland."

"You sure did watch a lot of television, for someone who hated it."

"All part of my cover. I wanted everyone to think I loved America." He flashed his teeth at me. "It was rather successful." He wrinkled his nose. "Pretending to be a nice man was not easy. I have some tastes that are rather, hmm, let me find the right word. Ah yes. My tastes are particular."

I'd watched enough true crime shows and read enough serial killer novels to know that this was not good.

I did not want Jace to get hurt, but I was getting nervous. My palms were sweating. My face heated up. My heart was pounding so loudly I felt it in my throat.

"Sit on the bed."

Should I resist? Fight him? Grab the gun?

Dimitri motioned with the knife. "You are a brave woman, Julie Teslo, but do not consider running."

I sat on the edge of the mattress. I had tucked a knife under the pillow earlier. Maybe I could reach it.

"I will make a souvenir for Jace to see when he arrives. It will enrage his beast. He will act rashly." He scraped the knife along my cheek. The blade was sharp but he didn't press hard enough to draw blood.

The knife on my face didn't stop. He traced a pattern of lines.

"You are curious, I see. I am tracing the Russian flag. In a moment, I will carve it into your face. You will not wear it long, because I will kill you." He cackled. "However, the bear will get the pleasure of seeing his lady with the flag of Russia written on her skin."

Okay, this dude was fucking crazy. Try as I might not to react, I had to admit, I was terrified.

Acid sloshed through my stomach as I tried to keep from jerking away.

I inched my fingers toward the pillow. He still had his gun, but if I could stab him in the heart, I might have a chance. He raked the knife across my other cheek.

I didn't move. I kept my spine perfectly straight. My heart was about to vibrate out of my chest, but I kept taking deep breaths. I was not going to give this asshole the pleasure of seeing me hyperventilate.

Dimitri spun the tip of the knife in a circle. It bore into my cheek. By now, it had probably drawn blood. "Now. Enough foreplay. I will now begin the flag to which I owe my allegiance."

My breath picked up.

Jace could get here any time with a long-range rifle and blow this joker's head off.

I pushed my fingers further toward the knife under the pillow. I was prepared to take my chances.

I closed my fingers around the handle.

Dimitri pushed the knife into my cheek and pulled.

I flinched. That was line one of the Russian flag. Straight into my cheek.

"Once this is done, maybe, I could go back to the former Soviet Union design. That one is so much more detailed. So much more powerful, yes?"

I wasn't going to end up with a fucking sickle on my face, even I had to die fighting it.

Glass shattered.

An almighty roar thundered through the cabin.

The table flew sideways as Jace, in bear form, flew through the window. Jaws open, teeth bared, he lunged at Dimitri. Jace knocked the gun from Dimitri's hand.

It slid under the bed.

Dimitri still had his knife. He slashed at Jace.

Jace lumbered backward, knocking into the table. Dimitri lunged.

I jumped up, skidding across the floor. I couldn't get close to the bed, and the knives Jace had left out on the table were scattered across the floor. I hated to admit it, but Dimitri's fighting skill with a knife rivaled any I'd seen before. I could throw them, but his reach technique was much better than mine.

Jace landed a blow to Dimitri's leg with a slash across his thigh.

But Dimitri countered with a stab to Jace's ribs. They continued, slashing, hitting, parrying, stabbing, clawing, in circles around the small living space.

Jace leapt onto Dimitri. They rolled, shoving the table. The legs snapped off of one of the chairs.

Dimitri brought his elbow back in a rowing motion and stabbed Jace until he let go.

Jace grunted, but he stayed upright.

After that brutal stab, Jace's movements grew less forceful.

Dimitri had grown tired as well. He crawled a few feet to use the wall to push himself up. But he didn't quit.

Jace cut a vicious line down Dimitri's back. But it wasn't over.

My eyes landed on the fire. If I could make a torch, I could use it against him. The poker! I grabbed the metal and shoved it into the fire.

While I let it heat, Dimitri continued to slash at Jace. Jace was moving slower and slower. A wound on Jace's shoulder grew. Blood trickled down to his paw and dropped onto the floor.

Jace swiped at Dimitri with his claws. Dimitri lunged with the knife.

I bounced on the balls of my feet while I watched the flames lick at the metal poker.

Hurry. Hurry. Hurry.

Jace's movements were slowing down even more. More blood coated the wooden floor.

Finally, the poker glowed red.

I held it tight with both hands. Dimitri ditched all of his gear before he started tormenting me, so he only wore a cotton henley. Perfect. If I could connect with his skin, Jace could get the upper hand.

I waited until Dimitri's back was to me. When Jace was mid-swipe, I shoved the poker into Dimitri's ribs.

Dimitri's shout rang in my ears. I shoved the poker handle harder.

Served him right for laughing at Ivan's reaction when I stabbed him.

Dimitri folded to the floor, clutching at his side, still screeching.

Jace took the opportunity I gave him. He launched himself onto Dimitri. He clamped his teeth into his shoulder and dragged Dimitri toward the door.

I yanked the door open. Jace dragged Dimitri through. He lugged his thrashing body across the snow and into the woods until I could no longer see them.

I pressed my hand to my cheek. It stung from the cut. My hand trembled as I swiped the blood off. The Russian flag, my ass. I was pissed, but also still shaky from the mind games Dimitri had tried to play with me. What would have happened if Jace had been a little later? Nope, wasn't going to think about that now.

There was plenty to do here.

I found a flat piece of plywood and propped it up over the window. I stuffed the open spaces with towels. I dumped a few more pieces of wood on the fire. I picked up the fire poker and gave it a pat. "Thanks for saving the day, fire poker."

Now I was talking to inanimate objects.

Just in case, I left it on the hearth.

My heart had not stopped thundering. My legs shook. I could barely take a step without my knees knocking together.

I was safe, but Jace was not.

I tried to banish the comment Dimitri had made about a rug from my head, but it kept bouncing back.

Where was Jace? I peered out the one remaining window. I could go help him. But I didn't have boots. If he wasn't back in five minutes, I'd go regardless.

I pressed my face to the glass.

Finally. After four torturously long minutes, there he was. His bear limped from the tree line. He staggered the last few steps toward the door. I pushed it open for him and he fell into the cabin. I rushed forward. I sank my hands into his fur.

Fuck. How could I help a bear?

"Jace. Shift back. Let me help you," I begged, letting him hear the fear in my voice.

He shifted. In the bear's place was Jace, covered in knife wounds. He got to his hands and knees.

"Are more of them coming? Jace. Are there more Russians?"

I would use Dimitri's gun on any asshole who dared get near us. Jace had saved me. I would defend us any way that I could.

"There's one more," he rasped, "but I didn't see or smell any sign of him on the way here. I thought he'd be with Dmitri. He paused. "Julie. You okay?"

I kissed his cheek. "I'm good."

He stumbled the last few feet and collapsed onto the bed. He reached for me, but as I grabbed for him, his arm fell limp to his side.

He was out cold.

I dropped to my knees. I laid my head on his chest for just a second.

He was breathing. Thank God.

I checked his pulse. It seemed weak for a man his size.

"Thank you for coming back to me." I pressed a kiss to his forehead. "I love you." The words had almost come out of my mouth several times over the last few days. I'd held them in. I wasn't going to hold them in anymore.

"I love you," I said again. I vowed to say it to him when he woke up.

He'd said he'd gotten them all… except for one. Although he could be coming for us now, there was nothing to do but wait out the storm. We were safe from immediate danger, for now at least. I had to focus on getting Jace through these injuries and sit tight. We'd deal with last spy, if he could survive the snowy coldness.

First, I would treat some of these cuts.

He had so many. I started at the top and worked my way down but I couldn't conceal my fear; his usually warm skin was clammy to the touch.

In a first aid kit, I found alcohol, peroxide, and bandages. I covered him with a thick blanket and started with his face. He'd said shifters healed faster than humans, but I had no idea how that would work with this much blood and these many wounds.

Outside, the wind howled. The door banged in its frame and the broken window definitely didn't help keep the draft out.

I let my head hang for a brief second. Not another storm. How much more could we survive?

I sucked it up and got to work. I wouldn't be the reason Jace didn't make it. One eye was swollen shut. I dabbed at it and a deeper cut crossed his cheek with peroxide. I smeared both with antibacterial cream and moved along, trying to address the worst of the remaining wounds first.

A deep cut crossed his neck, alongside the scar the real bear had given him. I cleaned it and taped butterfly bandages all down his neck, hoping they'd hold the cut closed until he healed. A needle and thread sat in the kit, but unless this didn't hold, I'd save the stitching for a doctor.

I became a pilot for a reason. This medical stuff is for the birds.

The injury on his shoulder was not a cut. He'd been shot. My own pulse picked up speed as I studied it. Jace told me he would survive a gunshot. I held onto that.

I knew enough to check the back of his shoulder, where I found an exit wound. Okay, that was good. I wouldn't have to dig a bullet from his arm. I cleaned it as well as I could and wrapped a gauze bandage around his shoulder.

Now for his chest. In the small amount of time I'd been tending to him, is skin had become colder and tinged with blue. A jagged cut swept down his pectoral muscle. I winced just looking at it. "That healing factor you claimed to have can kick in anytime now, Jace."

I cleaned it, cringing all the way down, taped it up, and put extra bandages on top.

Down his side, deep purple and black bruising covered his skin. His ribs had to be broken. My eyes stung. I moved to an extensive wound on his stomach. This time Jace flinched. That was a good sign, right?

As soon as we escaped this wretched patch of never-ending storms, I was going to redo my CPR certification and get some basic first aid training.

I kept working, treating every wound.

It took over an hour. When I was done, I checked his pulse again. It was still weak, but stronger than before. I stoked the fire and I lay down beside Jace.

"I love you. Make it through this."

The world needed Jace Branton. And maybe it was selfish, but I'd waited my whole life to find him. I wasn't going to lose him now. I wasn't above pleading with him. I kissed the one spot on his face that wasn't torn up from fighting.

"Please don't leave me."

JACE

I woke slowly. I was in human form and I was warm, lying on a soft surface. I felt like absolute shit. The hellscape of the last few days flooded back in.

"Julie!" I tried to push myself to my elbows. When I'd reached the cabin, I'd seen that freak Dimitri looming over her.

"Shh. I'm fine." Her hand stroked through my hair.

If I'd been more with it, I'd have realized that she'd pressed her heated body along my side.

I dropped my weight back to the sheets. She might say she was fine, but that kind of fear at the hands of another human being? It stayed with you.

When I saw her through the window with his wretched knife on her face, she'd been glaring up at Dimitri, tough as nails, as usual, sitting ramrod straight on the bed, but I'd seen the raw fear in her eyes.

I was eternally grateful that he hadn't killed her immediately. But I hated that he'd toyed with her. He was a sadistic monster. He hadn't just wanted her eliminated to save his own skin. He'd wanted to torture her. He'd have *enjoyed* it.

119

Revulsion burned my throat. I shuddered.

I'd probably never stop having nightmares about what could have happened. I blinked and turned my head, desperate to see her. My vision blurred as I tried to focus on her gorgeous face. Her soft lips brushed over mine. "It's okay."

It wasn't okay. I hoped it would be one day.

"How are you feeling?" she asked.

"Like hell. It's a hangover combined with being hit by a truck." I wiggled my arm. It was covered in tape. "Did you bandage these?"

"Every single one." She pressed her fingers to my wrist. "Your pulse is stronger. I think you're out of the woods." She snickered. "Literally."

"Always with the bear jokes."

I was touched that she'd taken the time to piece me back together, even knowing that I'd heal. She cuddled up to me and I closed my eyes again. I ran my hands over her. Her hair, her back, her arms. But when I got to her face, my hand hit a bandage.

How had I missed that?

"What's this?" I opened my eyes to see a flesh-colored bandage over her cheek.

"Dimitri's handiwork."

My throat felt like it was closing. I recalled the comments he'd made about Julie being naked, back when he attacked us in the cave safehouse. "What did he *do?*"

"Down boy. He's dead."

Getting air was hard. I sucked in a breath, not wanting Julie to see my panic. "I know he's dead. I made sure of it."

"Yeah?"

Had there been a doubt in her mind? I would not brag about my kill count on this mission. I hardly thought it would impress Julie. It might even repulse her. But I needed her to know this sick bastard would not be bothering her ever again.

"Yeah. His head is no longer attached to his body." I took no pleasure in killing, not most of the time. But with Dimitri, killing him had satisfied my bear.

"That'll do it."

Julie was still holding out on me. "Tell me."

"It's not important. It's over."

I switched tactics. "You need to talk about it to deal with it."

She gave me a pointed stare. "I will if you will."

"Fine." I couldn't suppress a growl. "Julie. Please tell me. It makes me sick not knowing what that freak did."

"Okay, but don't lose your mind over it."

I would most likely do exactly that.

She fixed her eyes on the ceiling, not making eye contact with me. "Freak was exactly the right word for Dimitri. He was a sadistic pervert."

My nostrils flared. I wanted to kill him all over again, but this time I wanted to take my time. "Did he touch you?" The thought that he could have hurt Julie like that because I was too slow sent icy needles through my stomach.

"No." She met my eyes. "Not like that."

I hoped she was telling me the truth. God, I should have been faster. I wasted so much time in the woods, not realizing Dimitri had raced ahead to torment Julie. "Then what did he do?"

"He wanted to carve the Russian flag in my skin. He wanted you to see it. Then he wanted to kill me."

The fucker wanted to hurt her. On purpose, for fun. "Oh god, Julie. I'm sorry. I'm sick that I wasn't there to protect you."

"You did protect me. You came barreling in, fur flying, and saved me."

"Not soon enough."

The icy needles in my stomach turned hot. Anxiety burned through my belly. Holding onto hatred wasn't smart. But moving on from what he did? Not a chance.

"Yes, absolutely soon enough." She took my face in her hands. "Jace. Look at me. You saved me. You probably saved a whole bunch of other people too. Those guns are in the hands of the military now and not with a bunch of spies who want to harm us."

Logically, she was correct.

I couldn't accept it. I should have been faster. Next time, I would make sure Julie was safe first. Plus I let one escape.

"Is any of this sinking in?" she asked?

It wasn't. But that wasn't her problem. She'd had enough to cope with.

"Yes. I love you." I pulled her back down to me. "Let's go back to sleep."

It wasn't her job to coddle me or soothe my feelings. I would deal with this on my own, without upsetting her. She deserved a break after what she'd been through.

For twelve more hours, the storm battered the little cabin. I slept for most of it, waking every so often to reassure myself that Julie was really in my arms.

I woke to her sprawled half on top of me. I pressed a kiss to her cheek. "Thank you for saving me last night."

I felt a little more grounded. I'd gained some perspective after sleeping. I was still crushed over the fact that Dimitri had planned to torture Julie before killing her and that he'd managed to leave a mark on her face even.

I reminded myself that I'd arrived just in time. As my mate, Julie would remain my priority. If she were in harm's way, I'd strategize differently. I'd make sure I knew where my enemies were before engaging. That's where I'd gone wrong last time. I'd let my bear fixate on killing all of them when I should have cut off the head of the snake. I knew better. Never let the leader go.

What had worked when I was single would not work when I had a mate.

I was a soldier. I would adapt.

I scooted closer to her. Still half asleep, she made a humming sound. She rolled off me and curled into a ball on her side. I followed her, pressing my body against hers.

She wiggled her bottom against my front.

"Someone's feeling better."

I hid my face in her long dark hair. I inhaled her unique scent. She tapped me with her foot. "Stop smelling me. I haven't showered yet. I didn't want to leave you."

I tightened my arms around her. I didn't want her to leave me now either. "Mmm. You always smell good. Like citrus and flowers."

"I doubt that."

"You're not allowed to argue with me while I'm incapacitated."

She rocked back against me again. "You don't feel too incapacitated to me."

"Because you cured me."

She spun to face me. "Seriously. How are you?"

"I'm not one-hundred percent, but I'm close." I bit her earlobe. "I'll be better once I'm inside you."

She tossed her head back. "Now that's something I won't argue with."

"How are you feeling?" I asked her. She knew what I meant. The cut on her cheek wouldn't have serious physical consequences, but it could have lasting mental ones.

"I'm okay. I don't know that I'll jump right into clinical

therapy, although it might be required once the post office finds out what happened. I'll probably end up talking about it with my grandmother first. Get my head on straight."

"As long as you're taking care of yourself."

"Does the Army require you to get counseling after a mission?"

"Yeah. We have a shifter that's trained in combat issues and PTSD."

"Makes sense. It would be hard to confide in someone if you could only talk about half of yourself."

I loved that she realized the bear was half of me, not just a tiny part.

"Enough of that," she said. She picked up where we left off, rocking against me.

I stilled her movements. "I need a shower first." I peeled a piece of tape off the cut on my chest. It had been particularly bad. I remembered the sharp bite of the knife and the matted fur wet with blood as I fought Dimitri. The cut had closed overnight, though the scar was still red and inflamed.

"Ouch," she said. She leaned in closer. "It looks awful, but a thousand times better."

"They should all be more or less okay by now." I pried more bandages off, crushing them into a little pile on the bed.

When I turned to speak to Julie, she had leaned forward with her head in her hands. I put my hand on her back. "You okay?"

She nodded. When she spoke, her voice was muffled. "Just thought I'd lost you for a while."

Last night she'd fended off a terrorist, a terrorist who'd intended to torture her. That alone would put even the most seasoned soldiers out of commission for a few days.

During a brutal fight, she'd given me an opening by using a fire poker on that same man. After that she'd patched me up, which couldn't have been pretty. Then, from what I had gathered, she'd sat up with me all night.

And I could barely think about it, but she'd faced Dimitri threatening to carve the Russian flag into her skin. Partly for his own pleasure, I suspected, and partly to get to me.

Again, I was struck by her resilience.

I rubbed my hand over her back and shoulders. There was nothing I could say, no platitudes that would help.

"I love you," I said.

I froze. I hadn't planned for those words to leave my mouth.

She let her hands fall from her face. She looked up at me, stunned. Her eyes were red, but her bright smile spread slowly across her face.

"Do you mean it?"

"Of course I do. What kind of question is that?"

"Just making sure." She beamed. "I love you too. Actually, I said it first."

"You did not."

"I did. Last night, when you were unconscious. I said it out loud. Right to your face."

"That does not count!"

"It does too! I think you must have been aware that I said it first, at least on some level, and that's why you said it back today. Because I paved the way."

"Oh my god. I cannot believe what I am hearing right now." It felt good to be silly for once. My love for her was not silly at all, but without the shadow of the Russians hanging over our heads, we were free to just hang out and tease each other.

She giggled.

"As soon as I can pick you up, you are going to get it."

"It's a date."

"I'm ready for that shower."

She sat up and held her hand out to me. I took it, though I outweighed her by close to a hundred pounds. I groaned as I got to my feet.

"Sore?"

"Oh yeah. But it'll go away as soon as I get in the shower with you."

Before we showered, I wanted the bed clean. I stripped the filthy sheet from the bed. I flung a clean blanket over the mattress. Now we wouldn't have to pause once we were finished letting the hot water wash all the grime from our bodies.

∼

As soon as we were dry, I lifted Julie and wrapped her legs around my waist.

She prodded one of the new scars on my arm. "Are you sure you should be holding me up in the air like this? What if you bust one of these open?"

"Holding you? I'll show you how well I can hold you," I growled. "I'm going to slide into you while I'm holding you up."

She moaned.

I gripped her with one arm. I held her steady with my left hand and found her opening with my right hand.

I gathered her slick heat with my fingers and spread it over her clit while she undulated against me. I moved my hand to my erection and stroked it. It was already hard, and touching myself was getting me too close. I dipped my fingers into her pussy. I gathered more of the slick wetness and spread it over my waiting manhood.

I pulled her up into the air, letting her hover above my dick.

Suspended in the air, I balanced her, then I pulled her

down, in one perfect thrust, I was inside. She enveloped me completely.

Riveted, I couldn't look away. I could see her perfectly. Her breasts bounced. Her stomach muscles pulled taut. Her pussy gripped me as I plunged in and out of her body.

"I love you," I said. I didn't think I'd ever tire of saying it to her.

"I love you too." She brought her hand down to meet the spot where our bodies joined. "Guess I shouldn't doubt what you can do with this fine body."

I'd also never get tired of hearing her lust after me. I squeezed my jaws together. The feathery light touch of her fingers on my erection while it thrust into her body was heady. "That's right. I can make you come, that's what I can do."

The grateful buzz I'd acquired after surviving Dimitri hadn't faded. I wasn't taking a single thing for granted.

I was very thankful, but I could still have a little fun.

Keeping a tight grip on Julie's ass, I walked us to the refrigerator. I opened the drawer where I stored a few bottles of beer.

Beer wasn't usually one of the staples I kept in a safe-house—it was not the best use of space—but this cabin had a fridge, and two weeks ago, the rest of my unit was here for three days. We'd been doing some recon during the day and amused ourselves with beer and poker games at night.

I pulled a bottle of Roughneck Stout from the drawer. I popped the cap off with my bare hand. I was still inside her and I was just as hard as I had ever been.

Julie hooked her ankles tighter around my waist. "What are you doing?"

I thrust up, pushing my cock into her sweet spot. "Just showing you how well I can hold you up."

"Jace!"

I lifted the bottle to my mouth. I took a long, slow drink. "Mmm. Good. I can taste the barley and a hint of vanilla." I held the bottle up. "You want some?"

She smacked at my chest lightly. "I cannot believe you!"

"You don't like beer? How about wine?"

She grabbed the bottle and turned it up, taking a long drink. "I like beer just fine." She made a big smacking sound with her lips and kissed me on the mouth before leaning back. "When your ribs bust into tiny pieces, don't blame me."

"Somethings going to bust, but it's not my ribs."

"Jace Branton. Well, I declare! The mouth on you."

I couldn't help it. At the sound of her phony southern twang, I laughed so hard she slipped a little along my length and I moaned.

She leaned forward and licked a long stripe up my neck.

"That tickles."

"It's supposed to."

"Doesn't matter what you do, I won't drop you." I kissed her neck. "The last time you tickled me, I ended up fucking you on the cave floor."

"Is that supposed to be a threat?"

"It's a promise."

I lay her on the bed. As much fun as the varied positions had been, nothing beat being face to face with Julie.

"I'm never going to get enough of you."

How was it possible that a week ago, I watched this woman from afar, unwilling to take a chance? I'd denied my bear a mate and denied myself happiness.

There was still the issue of whether my special ops unit or my family would accept that I had chosen a human mate.

If I was forced to choose between Julie and my family, or Julie and the military, what would I do?

The answer was simple. I didn't have to think.

I would walk away. I would leave behind my career and

my family to be with her. Julie was my family now and my bear agreed whole-heartedly.

With Julie, I could start over. I valued my service to my country. I loved my fellow soldiers. But there were other jobs, other careers. The sacrifice was worth it.

Julie was necessary to me and to my bear. Protecting her was my number one priority; everything else came in a distant second place to having her love.

I picked up her hands and kissed her palms. I kissed her stomach. I moved to her ankles.

"I love every single inch of you."

"Every inch?" Julie wasn't laughing now. She was smiling, but she looked breathless with desire.

She was everything I could have imagined wanting. We laughed together. She was tough as hell and brave. She didn't take shit from anyone and she loved the outdoors as much as I did. She also respected the shifter side of me.

I was damned lucky. And I was grateful. I wanted to make sure she knew it.

I pushed her legs apart. "I like seeing you like this." I shoved a pillow under her hips. "All spread out for me." I bent over her and captured her wrists in my hands. I pulled them up by her head. "Leave them here." Her arms stretched above her head put her breasts at the right height for my mouth.

Kneeling up, I stared down at her delectable body, stunned that it was all mine.

I growled the word, *"mine."* I raked my cock over her pussy. The pressure inside me was already building.

She held her hand clasped above her head. Every time she writhed, her breasts bounced in my face. I kissed them all over, stopping to lick each nipple while she thrashed on the sheets.

"Put it in me, Jace. Come on." She spread her legs further

apart.

I pushed in, all the way to the hilt. Then I pulled out. I was rock hard.

"Jace. Stay in! Please!"

I grabbed her legs and put them on my shoulders. Her tight pussy gripped my length in its entirety in this position. "You feel so good." I pressed back inside. I kissed her calf, her ankle, her thigh as I thrust.

Our adventure, horror filled as it was, had come to an end for now. I refused to let her go. I had to show her what she could have with me.

I brought my fingers to rub her clit. I began a rapid pace of thrusting in and out of her body. "You're always so wet for me. I love it."

"You're a good lover," she said. "But that's not why I'm always wet. I'm turned on because of you. You know how to use what the Lord gave you, but you pay attention to me and what I want. It makes me want you even more. I love you."

My heart soared. My stomach fluttered. My skin flushed. My bear, always demanding, was for once appeased.

"I love you too," I said.

As far as I was concerned, this moment could last forever.

Still naked, Julie wrapped the blanket around herself. She padded to the front door and cracked it open. "The sky is blue and the air is clear. I think it's time we blow this joint."

I joined her at the door.

I breathed in the fresh air. "I don't feel another coming anytime soon."

She made a squeaky sound when she saw me. "I can't with you walking around naked in sub-zero temps."

"It's twelve degrees Fahrenheit. Practically balmy."

"What's tropical to you then?

"Hmmm." I tapped my finger to my chin. "Thirty."

She whacked me on the forearm. "It's making me cold just looking at you."

"I thought you liked looking at me."

She gave me a little pinch on the ass. "Don't think I can't see that sexy look you're giving me, buddy. I always like looking at you. But not when the door's open."

"I can fix that." I shoved the door closed and kissed her. "I hate to break it to you, but there's no need for me to get dressed when I'm going to have to shift."

"Right. No car. No cell phone. No way out."

"I hate making you go back out in the cold again." I still hadn't gotten over watching her suffer from hypothermia on our last romp through the snow.

"I'll be fine. This time, I'll have the added bonus of no active head injury, some winter gear, and no one will be shooting at us."

It would be so easy to become morose and fixate on all of our problems. But Julie remained upbeat and cheery, no matter what.

"I love the way you look on the bright side. We're on the west side of Chatanika. It'll take a little less than an hour to get to Fairbanks if I run."

"I don't want you overdoing it," she said. "You almost died yesterday."

"I'm fine. And the same goes for you."

She shook her head. "I'm great. Just having a pair of gloves will make this a luxury compared to the last trip."

She cocked her hip as I got ready to shift. "If you're human and I ride on your back, do I call it a piggyback ride, or a bear back ride?" She dissolved into a fit of giggles. "Bareback! I made a pun!"

I shook my head. "I love you, but that was really bad."

JULIE

After one last semi-grueling journey, Jace stopped behind a log cabin on the north side of Fairbanks. I let go of his fur and hopped to the ground.

Finally.

Within seconds, he'd shifted and looked like a man again.

A very sexy, very naked man, which I was now allowed to look at.

"Get an eyeful," he said.

"I plan to." In fact, I never planned to stop. Jace's wounds were mostly healed now. Thin lines that had been deep cuts yesterday still ran over most of his body. Many looked like they'd fade completely. Some would leave permanent scars. The deep cut on his chest would scar and so would the gunshot wound in his shoulder.

They made him even hotter.

He was a brilliant fighter and a fierce protector. They made him look like what he was to me and to the citizens of this state: a hero.

The muscles in his back flexed as he reached for the backpack I'd worn on the ride over and pulled out a t-shirt and jeans. I ran my hand down his strong back to his firm ass. "I think you could stay naked."

He shot me a look full of promise. "Yeah?"

"Oh yes. One day soon we need to spend the whole day naked."

"Julie. If you keep talking like that, we'll end up back in bed. Which I would love, but we have so much to do first."

"I know. You're the responsible party here. Not me."

He laughed.

It was still such a pleasure to hear his joy after thinking he'd always be remote and distant from me.

"Hey, how does your cheek feel?"

I brought my hand up to the spot where Dimitri had left his mark. In the light of day, it was just a thin red line. In time, it would look like a scratch from a bramble bush. Not a cut from a sadistic Russian spy.

"It feels pretty good."

"I have some cream I can put on it. Our special forces unit uses it, but it works for humans too."

"I'll be happy to use it, but don't worry. If that's the only souvenir I have from this madhouse, then I'll deal."

"I still hate it."

"At least I didn't get shot. Like you did."

"Don't even mention that."

After he dressed, we made it to the cabin. The cabin was not as small as the other cabins we'd crashed in, and it had some extra amenities, such as a basketball hoop and an ATV parked under a shed. "Never thought I'd be so glad to see civilization. Another safehouse?"

"No. This is my house."

"Your house? Like the one where you actually live?" It seemed like I stumbled onto something new about him every minute we were together.

"Yep."

I blinked. Jace and I loved each other, but he was still so private. He hadn't said a word about bringing me to his house. I hadn't realized he had a residence. For all I'd known, he lived like a monk in the barracks, and kept as few belongings as possible.

This house wasn't impersonal at all. Now that I looked closer, it was full of character. Flowerbeds surrounded the edges, and a back porch led straight to a fire pit with six chairs surrounding it.

I flopped onto one of the lawn chairs. Maybe we could make a fire and roast marshmallows tonight.

"Lots of guests?" I was trying not to let it bother me that there was so much about him that I didn't know.

Jace took a seat right beside me. "Just the guys from my unit. Sometimes they bring their wives. A few have kids. They're all bear shifters, so they like to sit outside while the kids run through the woods."

Colleagues, wives, kids. All of that was a huge leap for me. I'd never even gotten to the meet-the-family stage with a guy before.

Nervous didn't begin to cover how I felt about meeting his unit. That was assuming that I met them. "Tell me the truth. Will I be a problem for them?"

If they were all as buttoned-up as Jace had been before I crashed my plane, I didn't foresee them wanting me around for any of their bonfire parties.

"It's complicated."

Wow, that did not help my anxiety over meeting, or not meeting, his special ops unit.

I swallowed hard. I felt a twinge in the pit of my stomach. Maybe I was unnerved for no reason.

"I'm Inuit, but also American. I get complicated. My family is okay with us dating non-Inuits, but they will grill you."

Jace's eyes clouded, but his face remained impassive. His look gave nothing away. "It's forbidden."

The twinge in the pit of my stomach turned into a full-on spasm. *Forbidden*? Was this the eighteenth century, or what?

"Ah well. Inuits can be a demanding set of in-laws, but it's not an absolute no, even with grandma. Is it the older set that get their panties in a twist over you seeing a human?"

"No, it's all of them. It's actually a clan rule: no dating humans. There are some ways around it though. There's a process for getting permission. I'll talk to the clan elders and update them. It won't be a problem."

Jace's tone was off-hand and dismissive.

Had he just blown off my concerns?

The pit in my stomach was now a gaping chasm.

I stood up from my deck chair. I stood in front of Jace with my hands on my hips. "It won't be a problem? What the hell?"

Jace stayed in his chair. It must be nice that he felt like lounging right now. Although I hadn't known him long, I knew him well. Something else was wrong and it was bothering him. And to make matters worse, he was still keeping it from me.

"I said I'll handle it."

He was *infuriating*.

"From the look on your face, there's more you haven't told me," I said. "What is it?"

Jace kept his voice even. "My situation is more complex because I'm with the special ops shifter unit."

"Do they forbid it too?"

"I'm not sure. We're not allowed to tell anyone, or reveal ourselves, so it hasn't come up."

How was I just now hearing about this? I did not keep my voice even. "Were you going to mention this at any point?"

"It didn't seem relevant while we were fighting for our lives."

Now I was full-on shouting. "Didn't seem relevant? Are you kidding me right now?" Was Jace really this clueless about human interaction?

Still, Jace remained in his chair as if he didn't have a care in the world. "I am not kidding. Six men were trying to kill you. That was my priority."

I crossed my arms. Jace's impassive face was still gorgeous in the moonlight. "I'd think your priority would also be telling me that you're not even supposed to be talking to me, especially before you fucked me!"

Jace worked his jaw a few times. "Do not cheapen what we have between us."

"You have a lot of nerve! You're the one who wasn't honest with me."

"I never lied to you."

"Right." I paced around the fire pit. "You just didn't tell me anything. I had to drag every single thing out of you."

Jace's eyes turned hard. He remained silent. He was not reacting. He was not mad. He was barely there. And that pissed me off, more than the fact that he omitted a huge fucking issue that would affect both of our lives.

"Don't tell me you're going to retreat and go back into silent man mode. I cannot deal with that!" I had to get the hell away from him. I needed a break before I said anything I couldn't take back. And I was very close to unleashing a righteous amount of fury all over his bear-shifter ass.

His face was stony as he watched me pace. "Where are you going?"

"Away."

"Julie. Do not walk away from me."

"Oh, that's rich." He did not get to tell me what to do. Not for one second. "Why not? I don't even know who you are."

I made it all the way into his house before he caught my arm.

I never heard him get up.

I didn't know bears could be stealthy, but Jace sure the fuck was. He held on with a firm grip but left it loose enough that I could get away.

His eyes were flinty. His mouth a hard line. But I was never scared of him. I was furious and hurt, but I still loved him.

I didn't want to get away. Not if he wanted to chase me. Chasing me was a much better option than if he'd stayed seated, cold and inaccessible.

"Julie. Stop trying to pull away from me. I know it's been a rough few days."

"Do not put this off on me like I'm falling apart because I'm a hysterical woman."

"Hey. I'm referring to both of us." His voice lowered. "I'm rattled."

"You are?" I stood with my mouth open. I hadn't expected him to admit any vulnerability, especially not out loud. My heart softened. It had probably cost him to be that honest with me this soon. If he was struggling, I didn't want to be the cause of that.

"Yes." He took both of my hands into his. "Now. You're going to listen to me while I apologize. I should have mentioned it. I didn't. I'm sorry about that."

Well, that took the wind out of my sails. I deflated. "How'd you get so calm about this?"

"I'm not."

Mad or not, I'd never get tired of hearing his deep voice, laced with sincerity. "Well, then how are you being so rational, while I'm running around and yelling?"

He didn't speak for a moment. I could tell this was like pulling teeth for him. He dreaded sharing himself and yet he was trying, for me, but I wasn't ready to put him out of his misery just yet.

"Jace?"

Jace wrapped his arms around my shoulders and we both walked back outside. I wondered if his bear felt better being out there under the stars when he was upset.

"My bear couldn't stand it. He couldn't watch you walk away."

So maybe this shifter thing could come in handy if we both knew how to handle it. "Well thank god for that."

Watching this big strong man, who was so handsome and giving, try to explain himself to me, when everything inside of him rejected it…it moved me. I loved him so much.

Jace pulled me into his arms and we stood there in the cold night air, embracing. "He wouldn't have let you leave. And I wouldn't have either."

"I wasn't going to *leave*. Just stomp around inside your house and maybe slam a door." How far would I have gone? I'd only planned to get into his house and maybe lock myself in the bathroom. Not the most mature move, but the idea of leaving Jace never crossed my mind.

"He didn't know that."

Wow.

"Thank you for telling me that." I sank into one of the campfire chairs. "So, I guess it's pretty obvious that neither of us has had a long-term relationship."

"Why is that?"

"Because we just screwed that up in a spectacular way. You didn't tell me something crucial to our relationship. And I completely spazzed out and didn't listen to you or give you a chance to explain."

"Let's look at the positives. We fought. We made up."

"You're right. And from what I hear from my myriad of married family members, these types of fights don't stop.

They keep right on coming, even forty years down the line."

I could only hope that Jace and I would still be together in forty years.

"Good point, and a practical outlook. We'll just have to learn to fight a little better."

I laughed. "Fight better. That's funny. But I'm still speechless. We might not even be able to date."

"Julie. You are my mate. If my commanding officer tells me we can't be together, then I'll leave the military when my contract is up."

Jace had killed for me.

He'd protected me in such a fundamental way. I could never repay that debt.

Killing was part of his job, but this time it might not have been. He might have found the spies and apprehended them. He had made me his priority over his career, but I hadn't realized he might have to pick one of us over the other.

"I don't want you to give up your career." It was clear that Jace's career was ideal for him. Just as I couldn't fathom it for myself, I couldn't imagine him caged, trapped inside doing an office job.

"In an ideal world, I'd have both. But you are more important. You are the most important thing to me." He sank down beside me. "I choose you."

Tears sprang to my eyes. I wiped them away quickly before they could run down my face. "I choose you too."

I recovered quickly from my sudden fit of emotion. I needed to call my family and my boss to let them know I was alive.

"My family is probably going crazy. No, scratch that, they're definitely going crazy." The sheer terror I'd felt while

Jace was gone came rushing back and I'd only known him for a few days.

I knew my parents and grandparents would be devastated. If the rest of my family had felt even a fraction of that, then I needed to quit jacking around and let them know I was alive. "I should call them."

I was not eager to see how they'd suffered. But I should end that suffering as soon as possible.

"I have a cell phone here." Jace disappeared into the cabin. He came back and silently handed me the phone.

I knew my mother's number by heart. She picked up immediately. Jace sat next to me and held my hand.

"Hi, mom."

"Julie!" My mom burst into tears. "You're alive! I knew it. Oh god." There were a lot of rustling sounds and distant voices. "Get in here! Julie's on the line!" She came back to the phone. "Where are you?"

In the background, a chorus of voices rose. I could hear at least a dozen family members screaming, crying and shouting.

"I'm in Fairbanks. I'm tying up some loose ends. I'll be home in a few days."

She gasped. "Days!"

"Yes. I promise I'll come home next week and stay."

"Julie. We were so worried. Where have you *been*?" The anguish was clear in my mother's voice, and although I hadn't done anything wrong, I still felt guilty.

"Long story short, my plane went down."

"Yes, we know that much. Someone from the post office came by with a State Trooper. They told us your plane was in pieces."

Oh god, I hadn't even thought of my job sending a formal notification to my parents. But it made sense considering the circumstances.

"We demanded a search and rescue," my mom said. "And they had one planned, but not until the storm ended. That would have been too late. We all went to the airport, but no flights were taking off. As soon as we could see five feet in front of us, we all started driving toward Wales."

My parents had taken off to try and find me. I had expected nothing less, and I was grateful they were safe and not lost out in the tundra looking for me. "Mom, there was nothing you could have done."

"You'll understand one day. If your baby was stuck out in the snow, you'd go too."

I had no doubt she was right. I'd have done the same for Jace.

"Where are you now?" I asked.

"We're in Talkeetna, trying to get a flight to Wales."

"I am so sorry, mom. Obviously, I'm fine and you guys can go home now." I pressed the phone closer to my ear. It was hard to hear with all the background noise from my relatives. "Who all came?"

"Everyone. Of course they did."

Oh lord.

"It's not your fault. But maybe you'll think about a new career. There's a fourth-grade teaching position open."

"Thanks, mom. I love you."

"Well, tell us where you've been this whole time that we've been going out of our minds."

"I was trapped in the plane first, then I was rescued by a special ops soldier out on a training exercise. We got stuck in the storm and we had no phones, no working vehicle, no way to leave or communicate. We just had to wait it out.

"I know that I shouldn't have been flying in the storm. I promise. I won't fly in bad weather again."

I wasn't sure how I was going to break it to them that I'd also fought a group of six Russian spies. One thing at a time.

I pressed my hands over the pressure points in both temples.

"Mom, can I call you back?"

"Yes. We can't wait to see you, honey."

I hung up the phone and sat back.

"You okay?" Jace asked.

"The post office and a state trooper came to see my parents. It was assumed I was dead. They all took off to try and rescue me."

"They sound like wonderful parents. With your can-do attitude."

"They're a lot. So very intense but I love them."

"You haven't met my clan yet. I think you'll have a new appreciation for the word intense." Jace had done a one-eighty. He'd gone from giving me nothing about his background to telling me what it would be like to meet his family.

Meeting a shifter clan was a much bigger deal than your normal meet-the-parents gig.

"What will your parents say?"

"I'll call them next week and find out."

"Will they be upset?"

"I don't think so," I laughed. "I think they'll be so happy that I'm dating and not a psychotic loner destined to be a forever-bachelorette, that they'll just deal with it."

Jace and I might never have a 'normal' dating life. And that was okay. But good lord. How much craziness could we stand?

"I think that we deserve to have a super calm relationship from here on out."

Jace kissed me hard. "I can get behind that."

JACE

I comforted Julie after her upsetting phone call with her parents, but I was still off-kilter from my fight with her. I would have much preferred to not reveal that much of myself. When we'd fought, I'd been stripped bare. The human side of me had been pissed off. I'd felt like she was overreacting.

After all, I'd told her about my family, just not right away.

Panic didn't describe the way my bear reacted. He wanted to shift and howl at her. Not to scare her, but to show his absolute anguish.

I'd convinced him that she wouldn't have seen it that way.

He left me to handle it as a human, but he wasn't happy.

His distress at seeing his mate walk away left me edgy. Clearly, I was going to have to get my shit together and learn to manage my bear when we fought.

No matter how long we were together, I still didn't think I'd ever let her walk away.

Julie seemed to sense that, either through intuition or observation. She plopped herself down in my lap in one of the big wooden campfire chairs.

I held her close.

She leaned her head back against my shoulder. I ran my fingers through her hair and kissed her mouth.

Finally, my bear settled.

I couldn't put it off any longer. It was time to face the music and call my commanding officer, which was actually the lesser of two evils. If the military didn't accept Julie, I could leave my career but my family and my clan would be harder to part with, but I'd do it. For her. After the horrors they've been through, they were even less open to shifters dating humans than before; it'd be my job to make them comfortable.

Julie had used my cell phone to wrangle her frantic family. Now there was no putting off the call to my boss. And then I'd call Luke. He'd take it the best and hopefully give me some guidance.

I sat outside on the edge of the back porch. For a difficult call, there was no way my bear wanted to be inside. I placed the signal jammer next to me, even though I was calling on a secure line.

As soon as I picked up the phone, Julie poked her arms through mine and wrapped herself around me from behind.

"Nervous?" she asked. Julie's arms tightened around my chest.

"No. Whatever happens, we'll be together." I didn't want to leave my unit. I'd miss serving every day. But I wouldn't regret it. I kissed her on the nose.

She squeezed my hand. "I'm going to give you some privacy," she said.

I squeezed Julie's hand, hoping she could feel my unspoken *thank you* in the gesture.

She walked into the house. I watched her go. Her borrowed pants hung loose on her, but I could still see the lovely shape of her backside.

It took everything I had to not chase after her instead of making this phone call.

He picked up on the first ring.

"Colonel Torres, Branton here."

"Branton. Good to hear from you. Give me a situation report." Bears didn't gravitate toward an alpha like some other animals, and neither did bear shifters, necessarily. Most bear shifters were loners although we do have clans and some clans had alphas.

The human part of me had come to rely on Colonel Torres as a human authority figure and a mentor instead of a leader whose word was absolute law.

"The good news is that I found the spies. The bad news is that they're all dead except for one."

"One escaped? Were you able to question any of them?"

"No. Unfortunately not." I had to clear my throat. I was having trouble talking. "They all attacked." I had given these reports hundreds of times. I usually rattled them off at light-ning speed and got on with the written part. Words had never gotten caught in my throat. "One managed to get away."

"Give me a run down."

"There were six total that I'm aware of. The lead was Dimitri Petrov. He had five agents with him. Their base was the customs outpost in Wales. It seemed to be a long-term infiltration from what I could tell."

"Were you seen on camera there?"

"No, sir." No, I wasn't because Julie had been the one to catch them. If it wasn't for her, I might still be searching for the spies.

I wanted this conversation over. "You'll find their Jeep outside Koyukuk. It's on the main dirt road. The Jeep will be on its side and it might be covered in snow. There are four bodies there, within a half-mile radius." Unless animals or the elements had interfered.

"We'll send someone to retrieve the bodies, canvas the area for the missing Russian and they'll go over the Jeep too. See if we can find any additional intel."

"The remaining body is in Galena, near the safe house. That body is probably not going to be in the best shape." I'd said enough out here in my yard. If I kept going, my bear was going to rebel and lose it. The phone would probably end up in shards on the ground.

Even though Julie was inside, there was a chance she'd overhear me. Julie was tough, but I'd have preferred she not have to relive the events of the last few days again quite so soon.

"Any idea where the remaining guy went?"

"No sir, I initially thought he'd be with Dmitri but he was't in Galena and I didn't catch wind of him after the Jeep crash. There's a chance he didn't survive the snow storm."

"Got it. Were you injured?"

"Minimally." A lie, but one he'd never know about.

"No need for medical?"

"No." Thanks to Julie, I was nearly healed.

"You sound like shit. Take some time. Report here in forty-eight hours."

"Sir, I'd like to request a week of leave." I still hadn't broached the topic of my bear having chosen a human as a mate yet.

"Fine. Good work stopping these crooks."

"Thank you."

While I was planning the best approach to talk to him about Julie, my CO continued with instructions. "You know we operate off the grid, so technically your unit was on a peace-keeping mission in Peru this week and you were on leave. You know the drill; call the sheriff's office and let them know there was an incident. Make it plausible."

"I will sir." It was now or never. "There's something I need to talk to you about."

"Go on."

"I met my mate." There, I'd said it out loud.

"I'm guessing she's not a shifter."

"No, sir."

"Civilian?"

"Yes."

"Alright. I'll be honest, you didn't make things easy for yourself, Branton." He paused. "There's a process for this. I'll meet with your mate and we'll go over all the non-disclosure information."

"She's already aware that I'm a shifter."

"Explain." Colonel Torres's tone was curt.

"I'm sure you're aware of the seaplane crash near Wales." The memory of Julie's broken plane would haunt me forever.

"I am."

"That was her. The spies shot her plane out of the sky."

"Oh boy." His sigh was long and drawn out. "I see what you mean. We'll make the official story that bad weather caused the plane to crash. But we're going to have to reveal the Russian part too. We'll downplay their role. I'll contact her boss at the post office." My boss took a sip of something. I imagined I'd made him pour himself a stiff drink.

"Be here in one week. Bring your woman with you."

"Sir, is it going to be a problem? That I'm dating a human?"

"Not unless she's a Russian spy."

"Point taken, sir."

"As long as we can do some background checks and inter- view her, it shouldn't be an issue," Colonel Torres said.

"I will be present for Julie's interview." If they thought

they could interrogate her alone in a room, I'd grab Julie and we'd haul ass to Mexico.

"I won't stop you. Jace, relax. This isn't a trial. Let me tell you something." My boss's voice dropped. "My wife is a human."

I let that sink in. Never in a million years had I anticipated that my colonel's wife was human. How many more of us were carrying that secret? "I had no idea, sir."

"I didn't want you to have any idea. And I don't expect that to go any farther than you."

"No, sir, it won't." At this point, I wouldn't even tell Julie, not until I had permission. I figured I'd crossed enough boundaries for one day.

"I do recommend that you tell your unit. I'll talk to them too. No one else needs to know."

I lay back on the porch. The stars looked a little dimmer here than they had in Koyukuk, but they still blazed brightly.

"Are we good?"

"Yes sir."

"See you next week."

My commanding officer knew I had a mate. A human mate. And he understood because his mate was human too.

Now it was time to call my cousin Luke. He wasn't the head of our clan but he certainly held sway with the elders. Our conversation was short and to the point. Never one to mince words, he made it abundantly clear no one would be happy with me being mated to a human. In our clan, it's one thing to date, it's another to take an outsider as your mate. Technically there *was* a process to get elder approval but, it's never been done before. But then he surprised me by saying his mom signed him up for a matchmaking service, and he'd been matched with a human too.

I was blown away. How many more surprises could this week hold?

Jarred by yet another major revelation in the last few days, I lay on the porch steps until I heard Julie's footsteps.

I pushed myself up, not wanting to appear weak in front of her. I knew she'd say that if we were going to be partners, true partners, that I would need to share all of myself with her.

I didn't disagree, but some things were too ingrained to change.

After all she'd been through, it was my job to be strong for her. I'd worried about the impact talking to her family would have on her, but she appeared chipper.

"How'd it go?" I could hear the worry in her voice.

"It went better than I'd hoped. My commanding officer was supportive of us being together. Shock of my life."

Julie leapt into my arms. "That's wonderful."

"But we still can't relax. He wants us to call the sheriff and update them."

Julie bit her lip. "I can do that. But before we deal with the sheriff, I need a tour of your house."

"A tour?"

"Yes! We've been here for an hour and I'm still on the porch."

Hospitality was not my strong suit.

She ran her hand down my chest. "I haven't seen the bed."

The bed sounded like the perfect place to start and finish. "No, you have not." I went to lift her but she pushed back against my arms.

"We can't. Not yet. If we start, it'll be another two hours before we call the sheriff's office."

"They aren't important."

"They are too. You know they are."

"Not as important as me getting my time with you." I

wanted to be alone with Julie, but she was right. There was another call to make. Now that I could prevent it, I wasn't going to let any humans endanger their lives or even waste their time by sending out a search and rescue party.

Reporting incidents to the local authorities was tedious.

But because a civilian was involved, my special ops unit would let the local police or sheriff's office handle the investigation. If possible, the shifter special forces kept a low profile.

"Alright, honey, you take the lead on this one." I picked her up so her mouth was close to mine and kissed her.

I sat her gently back on the floor where she grinned up at me, showing off the dimples I adored.

"Honey? That's new. I think I like it."

"Yep. Because you're as sweet as honey."

Her cheeks turned a bright red. "Don't think I've forgotten how you first used that."

"Oh, I don't intend to let you forget." I would never forget our time together in the cave when she'd let me taste her.

I kissed her on the lips again. "I can't wait for us to be done with all this red tape. I'm sorry you have to deal with this part. I'd prefer to leave you out of it."

"Oh let me at 'em," she said. "I told you the Inuits are good at storytelling. I'll have them so wrapped up in the drama they'll forget to dig too deep."

"If you insist."

I was happy to let her do her thing, if that's what she wanted. I worked well in the military, but outside of my unit, my family, and now Julie, I'd rather avoid people. I wasn't used to concealing my identity either.

It didn't take long for two deputies from the sheriff's office to show up, one male, one female. They were friendly and a little baffled at hearing about the six Russian spies.

I let Julie spin a yarn and I listened, memorizing each part of the story. True to claim, she was a good storyteller.

The deputies listened intently as she detailed each part of the story, changing the parts where I was a bear. She also added in a few extra all-terrain vehicles into the story, to explain how we travelled over such a long distance in harsh weather.

Near the end, the male officer squinted at me. "Now how did you—just one man—manage to take on those six Russians?"

Until this point, I'd barely spoken. "I used an ambush tactic. I concealed myself behind a group of trees while they were in the Jeep. I used the element of surprise to get the upper hand. I learned the technique during combat training at Fort Wainwright. But all in all, we were pretty lucky." I'd have to hope that throwing some jargon at them would suffice. I also failed to mention one of the spies remained possibly at large. That information was for special ops knowledge only, for now at least.

Julie nodded, her smile full of fake earnestness. "Yes. We were lucky."

"Thank you for your service, Captain Branton. And Ms. Teslo, thank you for your cooperation. We're very glad you made it through."

The officers seemed satisfied, and they were both in awe of Julie, which I fully supported. Finally, they were gone, and I had my mate to myself once again.

"I think it's going to be hard to get used to sharing you," I said. "I got used to having you all to myself."

My bear rumbled in agreement.

JULIE

I fell to the floor in a mock heap.

"Oh my god! I have never been so glad to be rid of other people!" I rolled over to my back and stared up at Jace. "I do not want to talk to another person for a really really long time."

I thought I was an extroverted people-person. But after answering the invasive questions from my family, Jace's commanding officer, and the two deputies, I was on sensory overload.

"I have a proposal," Jace said. He joined me on the floor of his kitchen.

I know he didn't mean *that* kind of proposal. It was way too soon, and I wasn't sure if shifters got married in traditional ceremonies or not.

Would there be a proposal in my future? I'd never thought I was a person who'd commit a lifelong bond. But meeting Jace had changed everything.

If he asked, someday in the future, my answer would be yes.

"I want to take you to my cabin near here."

"Another cabin? Why don't we stay here?" I was a little iffy on whether or not I was a fan of cabins these days.

"Because my special forces unit knows I'm here. They drop by, anytime day or night. They're not used to me having any company."

"You better get some new locks then. And some boundaries." I stretched my arms into the air. "The cabin sounds good; I'm in favor of your colleagues and friends not walking in on me naked."

He growled. "That will not happen."

"Possessive much?"

"Are you just now noticing that?"

"You better believe I noticed. I liked it."

"I will be texting them to let them know I'm bringing my mate to the cabin. They will respect that, and steer clear."

"They'd better. Or else." I shook my fist in the air. I pecked him on the mouth. "You said we'd drive; how will we get there?"

"I have a Jeep here."

"Whew." I hoped he wasn't offended. Was that a thing? Would Jace be hurt that I wanted to travel in a real car? Or would he always prefer me to ride on his back?

"Not wanting to ride on my back again?"

"That sounded kinkier than you probably meant."

"I'll show you kinky."

I lifted one eyebrow. "I look forward to that. But seriously, no offense. Riding on your back was pretty cool, but my skin is still dry and peeling from our last foray into the open air."

He took me by the hand and we walked, arm in arm, to the carport. "This is my Jeep."

I put my hand on the souped-up black vehicle with giant

tires. "I like it. Lots of room for our skis." Now that would be fun. Me skiing, with Jace racing along beside me as a bear. "Hey, can you be my ski lift in the off-season?"

He shoved into me playfully. "I thought you were tired of riding on my back."

"Obviously, it comes in handy." I hopped into the passenger seat. "I'm ready when you are."

"We'll stop at the store on the way and get whatever you need. Otherwise, it's not the typical safe house. It's fully stocked, with a hot tub, and a sauna."

"Any spies?"

Jace made a rumbling growling sound. It came from deep in his chest. "None of those."

I'd never tire of that primal sound. "Very nice. I have to say that not having Russians barge in is a pretty big bonus."

"It's not the beach, but we'll have some privacy."

"I don't mind if it's not the beach if I'm with you." I hung my head. "Good lord that was sappy."

"Sappy, but true, at least on my end." He picked me up and swung me around. "I'm happy when you're happy, honey."

I threw my head back and laughed. "I'm guessing that means your bear is happy too?"

"He's ecstatic. He loves you."

"I love you too, Captain Branton." I jumped into the air and wrapped my legs around Jace's waist. "Why don't we test out this Jeep?"

*Thank you for reading **Special Forces Bear Shifter Mate**! Find out if Jace and Julie's love can survive meeting the clan in the next book, **Single Dad Matchmate**. Jace's cousin Luke Thomas is the Sheriff in the small town of Pine River, Arkansas, whose family hires a matchmaker to get him back in the saddle after a terrible* *breakup. Unfortunately, they weren't counting on him falling for a human from the big city. Will his newfound love Victoria be able to handle a family full of shifters?*

GRAB IT NOW

Or Keep Reading for an Excerpt

SINGLE DAD MATCHMATE

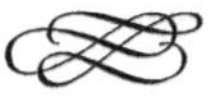

How many times would I tolerate a man answering his phone during a date? One? Two? How about six?

I swirled my glass before taking a sip. At least the merlot was good. The interruptions might have been excusable if my date was a surgeon. Or a therapist. Or even a professor, counseling students near finals.

But this man wasn't any of those things. He was a financial advisor, perpetually on the hunt for new clients. As a business owner myself, I understood the urge. But this had become excessive.

Now off the phone, he grinned at me through a mouthful of kale salad. "I see one of my clients over there. I'm going to go say hello."

I stabbed my fork into a piece of Tuscan-Style roasted asparagus. If I didn't have my reputation to consider, I'd walk out now.

Unbelievable. My so-called date led his client back over to our table. "Victoria, I'd like you to meet the owner of—" I tuned him out as he droned on, but I managed to refrain from crossing my arms. I smiled in the right places and offered my hand.

This date was a dud. He was another dull, pale-faced, self-obsessed businessman wearing a tailored suit. If he could stare lovingly at his phone on a date, so could I.

I sent a quick text to the newest number I'd saved in my phone: *I'm ready. I need your first available appointment. ASAP!*

Located in Midtown Manhattan, the agency was not what I expected. The inside of the office looked like a residence. The owner came out to meet me immediately and pushed a mimosa into my hand.

She caught me staring at the couches and dining table. "We didn't want Victory Matchmaking to feel like an office. We wanted it to feel like a home," she said. For the $25,000 fee, I figured she was right.

She ushered me to a sofa. "Tell me about what you want. None of this will leave the room. I'll make notes, but I'll write them as my interpretations."

The citrus was bitter on my tongue as I swallowed. "I don't know how to say what I want without sounding like a judgmental harpy."

She leaned in toward me. "You are here to get what you want."

How shallow was I going to sound when I admitted the truth of what I was looking for? "I know it's not PC, but I want an Alpha man. I don't mean one that dominates in the boardroom. I mean one that can throw a punch and shoot a gun."

She scribbled some notes. "I'm getting the picture. Tell me more."

"I want someone taller than me. I want a man who can

chop wood, and hammer a nail. I don't want him to be a selfish jerk, but I want to be able to tell the difference between him and my friends." I rubbed my hand over my face. "God, speaking of friends, they would be mortified to hear me saying these things."

She leaned in even closer. "I'd bet some of them secretly want the same thing."

"No." I had watched them over the years. I wasn't like them, not at all. "They want workaholic doctors, lawyers, and accountants. They want their husbands to pay for vacations, nannies, and private school." I sighed and dropped my head back on the sofa. "I fund my own life. I don't need a man to do it for me." I straightened back up. This was no time to lounge around. "I want a partner that I feel passion for. You'd think I could find him myself in a place like New York City."

"People hire you because you're an expert in web design and media. Let me be the expert in this." She gave me a firm tap on the knee. "I can find the right man for you," she assured me.

I picked up my pen. "Show me where to sign," I said. If she could find me the right match, this would be worth every penny. I was done wasting my time with losers.

The flames were out, but thick smoke billowed in front of me. I held on tight to the woman I carried over my shoulder. Just a few more steps, and we'd be outside. Ten steps later, I staggered into the fresh air, sagging with relief as the paramedics took her from me.

I groaned as I leaned my head against my SUV and took a deep breath. But just one, because I had to get my kids to a birthday party. Which was the very last thing I wanted to do after working for ten hours.

My real job was serving as the Sheriff of Pine River, but I also worked as a volunteer firefighter, along with a good portion of the rest of my family. Today an electrical fire had trapped two employees in a storage closet at the hardware store. They were safe, thank God, but it was close.

I thought about resigning at least twice a day. But the fire department needed me—most employees were replaceable, but a shifter firefighter wasn't. As shifters, we could move faster and lift more than the average person. If I could respond to a call, it might save a human. A human who was my kids' teacher, doctor, or friend. How could I say no to that?

After a short drive, I was finally home, or close to it. I stopped by my sister's house to collect the kids. "Daddy!" my kids screeched as they piled on top of me. "It's time for the party!" My daughter Beth yelled at the top of her lungs.

"They ate lunch," my sister Jane said. "We had pork chops and mashed potatoes."

I hugged her tightly. "Thank you. One day I'll repay you for this."

"Nah. I like it that you owe me." She punched me in the arm. "You know we're all in this together."

That was one benefit of the bear clan. We all lived on the same street, and we all had each other's backs, rain or shine, whether we enjoyed it or not.

And I hated to admit it, but I did need their help. My hours as sheriff were always uncertain. I'd officially retired from my first career as a soldier in special forces, made up only of shifters, but a few times a year the Army called me back to help my MASK.

I missed my MASK unit. But the travel was non-stop, and I had the kids now. The job came with some significant risks, and the kids were already down one parent—they didn't need to lose the only one they had left because I couldn't let go.

"Let's go guys, we've got to hurry." I grabbed a kid under each arm and hauled ass to the party, which was to celebrate my daughter's friend turning seven. In the birthday kid's backyard, every single thing was pirate-themed. The hostess was handing out eye patches for everyone, even the adults. It was a fucking madhouse.

Sure I had extra stamina as a shifter, but I was beat. I bowed out of socializing and slept in the car for two hours. After it was over, Beth bounced into the car. "Dad! Do you think we can have a mom?" she asked as she buckled her seat belt.

"Yeah!" Adam added as I helped him with his booster seat. "Moms make stuff like that. Tony said his mom's making a monster truck themed party!"

What the hell? He was five, and he knew about party themes? I didn't even remember being five.

Another unanticipated consequence of single-parenting —I sucked at crafts or whatever this would be classified as. I wasn't sexist enough to think it automatically fell to the mom. But they did seem to be the ones that made the fun stuff happen. I'd managed exactly one party for the kids. We'd only invited family, but even with cousins, we'd had fifteen kids. I'd texted them to be at the local pool at 2 p.m. and I'd shown up with a cake. I felt like I did a damn good job.

"Guys, moms aren't just for doing stuff that you want," I said. I backed the car up and started the path back home. "Moms are just like dads. Their job is to love you and take care of you."

"Yeah, like Aunt Jane!" My son chimed in. "Except Aunt Jane wrapped all of our presents to look like snowmen at Christmas."

I stared at Adam's hopeful face in the rearview mirror. On Christmas Eve, I had gotten off a double shift. I'd stuffed every gift inside bags. My mom and sisters would have been happy to take over and come wrap my presents, but I already depended on them so much. I wanted to be able to handle our family on my own, as much as I could.

"You guys really want a mom around? For real?" I thought kids didn't want their parents to date? Maybe that would be true if they had a mom they saw half the time. Instead, thanks to the nutcase I'd mated with, they had no mother at all.

"Yes!" They shouted in unison.

"What if she makes you eat broccoli every day? What then?"

"You make us eat it, Daddy!" Adam said.

Not very successfully. "Hmmm. What if she makes you clean the toilets with your hands?" I asked as I pulled into our driveway.

"She wouldn't!" Beth pounded the back of my seat. "It's not like *Cinderella*, Daddy! You would pick a nice lady!"

I didn't do such a great job the first go around. I promised myself I wouldn't bash my ex to the kids, no matter how tempting. When I was with my family or friends, all bets were off. If I had a few beers in close succession, I called her some pretty creative names.

I opened the door to the backseat to let the kids out. "She might! What if… she tickles you all day, like this?" I grabbed each kid and flipped them upside down. I was done discussing my love life with my kids.

By 9 p.m. the kids were asleep, and I was alone. No one to talk to, no one to watch TV with, and no one to sleep with. I didn't miss my ex, not really. She sucked for leaving her kids —there was no way to sugarcoat what she'd done. But I did miss having another adult in the house.

Maybe dating wouldn't be such a bad idea.

The next day the entire family got together to swim at the lake. I dumped a few dozen hot dogs onto the grill. "The kids want a mom," I said to my mother.

"They're right." My mom tapped me on the chest. "Those cubs do need a mom."

I looked over at my kids where they were digging in the sandy dirt with their cousins. "I thought I was doing fine."

"Luke Thomas. You know that is not what I meant," my mom scolded. "A grandmother and two aunts are not the same as a mother, no matter how invested they are." My mom's eyes widened. She clapped her hands together. "I know just the person."

Oh good Lord. Why had I told my mother? The air was cool enough, but between the heat from the grill and my mother's meddling, my temperature was about a thousand degrees. "Mom, please don't set me up on any dates. I don't want it to get awkward." Like the time one of the preschool teachers was interested. Or the mom of one of Beth's friends. Or one of the female firefighters.

My mom added a few more hot dogs to the grill. She never thought we had enough food. To her credit, feeding a sleuth of bear shifters was not an easy task.

"I'm not setting you up on a date," she said, squeezing my arms. "There's a professional matchmaker in Fayetteville. I just saw it on the news! And I know her."

I rammed a fork through one of the hot dogs at the edge of the grill. "A professional matchmaker?" I wiped the sweat from my forehead. "What the hell—is there a degree for that now?"

"She has a degree in sociology and psychology, and a master's in social work. She understands human behavior."

A breeze drifted by, but it did nothing to help me cool my heated skin. "I'm not human."

"Well any woman you meet most likely will be."

"If you think I need therapy, just say so." I wasn't opposed to that. I'd gone after a few brutal missions when I was working with my MASK unit.

"Would you please listen? She's not a therapist. She matches you with a compatible woman. It's much more reliable than a blind date."

I scooped all the hot dogs off the grill. I had to get away

from my mom before she had a wedding planned for a non-existent wife.

"If you found someone, she could help with the kids," my sister said, laying her chin on top of my shoulder.

I jumped into the air. "Where did you come from? Were you eavesdropping?" I whacked my sister with a spatula. "And that is not why I'd date."

My sister stuck a piece of cheese in her mouth. "Just sayin'."

It sounded like a fucking nightmare.

"Give it a try. What could it hurt?" Jane said.

It could hurt a whole lot.

I hadn't exactly agreed to see the matchmaker. In fact, I gave my mother a very definite no.

But my mother, sister, and sister-in-law all showed up on Tuesday morning, beaming. They promised my kids a trip to the park, ice cream, and roller skating. So on my only day off, I drove to Fayetteville to pay someone to find me a date. Just how I wanted to spend my free time.

I did consider the fact that if I got remarried, it would probably make my family's life easier. They'd feel less pressure to make sure the kids had a female presence. They tried to fill in for my ex—they showed up for class parties, fundraisers, and soccer practices. I was present as often as possible, but as sheriff, I was constantly getting called away.

How pathetic was it to have to pay for a date? This matchmaker would probably think I couldn't get one on my own, whereas the opposite was true. I knew it sounded arrogant, but quite a few women had pursued me since my ex bailed. This wasn't my own opinion, but I'd had at least six women tell me I was a catch, simply because I wasn't afraid of commitment, I was hard-working, and I liked kids.

I could not believe I was doing this.

Buck up. It's for your kids. You walk into burning buildings. You've run covert operations in deadly locations. You can face a matchmaker.

The matchmaker already had the door open when I got out of my car. "You must be Luke!" Her smile was wide. "I was so excited to hear from your mother."

Here goes nothing.

VICTORIA

"I have found the perfect man for you," the matchmaker said as she peered at me over her glasses. "However, I don't want you to immediately discount him because of his location."

Another day, another mimosa at Victory Matchmaking. This one was sweeter rather than bitter. "Now I'm curious."

"He's in Arkansas," she said, speaking quickly. "If you'll give it a chance, then--"

I held up my hand. I didn't need someone to convince me the south could be a decent place to live. "I'm from south Arkansas. My grandmother lived in Fayetteville. I spent a lot of time there growing up."

She adjusted her glasses and blinked at me a few times. "You're from Arkansas? I had no idea."

"No one does." At least she was too professional to make the usual jokes about me having all my teeth and wearing shoes. And she didn't comment on my lack of accent. I didn't work to drop my southern twang because I was ashamed. I dropped it because I wanted clients to focus on my work, and not the way I talked.

169

She handed over a sealed folder. "He's thirty-four. He's a former military officer. He's currently the elected sheriff in Pine River, a volunteer firefighter and he has two children, ages five and six. His ex-wife has no contact. He does have a lot of extended family living in the area, and he owns his home."

She stopped short of actually telling me his name. She explained the agency prefers to remove the temptation for clients to internet stalk their dates before meeting them. They find it makes the clients more receptive to their matches. Although it irked me slightly, I understood sometimes too much information can be a bad thing.

It sounded like she'd made this guy up for me. I was a little nervous about the kids, but not opposed. "When do I meet him?"

"As soon as you're ready. The agency will set up a plane ticket and hotel for you." She kept talking, explaining the process for the first date, but I couldn't focus. My mind skipped ahead. I didn't want to fly down to Arkansas, spend the weekend with a guy, and then come back to the city. I wanted a change in my life.

A very big change. "You know what? Go ahead and make the arrangements. But don't get me a return ticket. This is going to sound crazy, but I'm going to go stay in Arkansas for a while. I could use a break from the city. I'm going to give this a shot."

Her eyebrows shot up. "Ah. Okay. I didn't expect that. But we will certainly do whatever we can to accommodate you."

Thank goodness this was confidential. I would not be telling anyone else I was moving, however temporarily, to another state to go on a date with a man I'd never met.

Because that was one-hundred percent crazy.

If any friend of mine told me she was moving for a blind

date, I'd stage an intervention. I'd call her family, her friends, her co-workers—anyone I could think of to make her stop.

But Luke was only a small portion of my motivation. When I moved to New York City, I'd loved everything it had to offer. I took nothing for granted. Not the theater, or the museums, or the opportunities. But the life I lived now was nothing like that. I worked, and I went out.

I was sick of the social engineering. Of the jockeying for party invites. I didn't want any more dinner parties or weekends in the Hamptons or ferry rides to Nantucket. I didn't want to attend a gala, or sit on a board.

I wanted a normal life, like the one I had growing up. I wanted a family, with kids that I drove to school each day. I didn't want my future kids on a waiting list—since birth—for a Kindergarten where the moms wanted to one-up each other. I wanted to come home to a house with a swing set, and I wanted to go for a bike ride, or to a movie on a date night with the father of my children.

New York City could be a great place to raise a kid, if that's what you wanted. But I needed a break. That evening, it struck me as I packed my bags that I had nothing to care for here. No pets. No plants. No partner. No children. I'd hired the right people to run my company while I was away, and it really was time to go.

I might not have anyone depending on me directly, but I did owe Aria a phone call. My Director of Operations kept me on track when my left brain overpowered my right, and I locked myself away creating designs, instead of managing a company. She kept an eye on every department, and brought some of my pie-in-the-sky ideas back down to earth. Without her, our profits wouldn't be nearly so high.

"What's up, boss?" she said over the speaker.

"Hi, Aria. I'm going out of town for a while."

"The conference in Paris isn't until August. Wait." There was a loud scuffling sound as she picked up the phone. "Are you going on vacation? I'm going to forbid you from taking your laptop. You know we have it covered."

"It's a working vacation. I'm going home to Arkansas for a while."

"But your parents are in Canada."

"Yes. I saw them last month."

"So..."

"Are you trying to ask me why I'd willingly visit Arkansas?"

"I didn't say that..."

I laughed. "Arkansas is wonderful. The landscapes are breathtaking, the people are nice, and there are very few crowds anywhere."

We chatted for a few more minutes about specific projects we had open, and then we said goodbye. I was in a daze on the way to the airport, and while waiting to board. I couldn't believe I was about to leave the state for a man. But I wasn't turning back now.

I cleaned out my inbox and left an out-of-office message on my email and voicemail, but I checked my email one last time before the plane took off.

There was one email, from my CFO. She usually stuck to our office Slack program for sending me messages. Maybe Slack was down. I'd go ahead and read it before I was unavailable for a few hours.

Hi Victoria,

I've attached the notes from our strategy meeting, i.e. expanding our non-profit charity scholarship program. Let me know what you think.

We just met yesterday to discuss expanding our scholarship program for girls who were interested in web development. I clicked on the attachment, eager to see the summary of our meeting, and any other ideas she'd had. Odd. It wasn't the notes from the strategy meeting. It was an article—a lovely write up highlighting the rapid growth of our company, with details about our recent expansion.

She must have attached the wrong document, which wasn't like her at all. I'd have to ask her about it later.

For now, I had three hours to relax and drop my NYC mindset before embarking on this new adventure.

In Pine River, I found a charming restaurant called Apple Pie Diner. Or it was lovely until it caught on fire. Right as I bit into their spicy chicken sandwich, I smelled smoke.

A second later, two waiters shoved the doors open. "Get outside! Go! Run!" they screamed.

I didn't run, but I did go to the patio. Above the roof, a thin line of gray smoke hovered in the air.

A truck yanked to a stop in front of the building, and a man wearing full firefighting gear, minus the helmet, jumped out of the truck. He was stunning, even with the thick gear on. His brown hair was full, his jaw was strong, and his skin was a pretty tan, with just a little scruff on his face. My eyes met his as he pushed his way into the building. He was back out soon after, but this time he grabbed a ladder from his truck.

A few minutes later, an ambulance arrived, along with a car that said sheriff on it. The men and women that raced inside were all fit and gorgeous, though not one compared to the first firefighter.

Eventually, that first firefighter appeared. He raked his hand through his thick brown hair. A little soot was streaked across his handsome face but it only added to his looks. If this was how the men were made in Pine River, then my move to Arkansas was worth it, even if I only looked and never got to touch.

GRAB IT NOW

ALSO BY JADE ALTERS

What Could Be Worse Than Getting into a Love Affair with the Wrong Expectations? Love is Love But Sometimes You Just Have to Be in the Right Mood…

Studly Shifter Romances filled with Action, Adventure, Redemption and Second Chances

Special Bear Protectors:

Special Forces: Bear Shifter Mate

Single Dad Matchmate

Claimed by a Beast

Military Matchmate

Alpha's Second Chance

Chosen by the Clan

Bear's Fake Marriage

A Mystical World of Phoenix Shifters and Fantastic Creatures

Burnt Skies:

Phoenix Hunted

Phoenix Found

Phoenix Rejected

Phoenix Prince (Prequel)

Magically Delicious Mayhem

Reapers of Crescent City:

Reaper's Mark

Vampire's Desire

Psychic's Temptation

Mermaid's Call

Warlock's Claim

Historical Paranormal Romance

Secrets of Storyville

A Countess Betrayed

A Harlot Betrothed

Epic World Building Academy Romance

The Broken Academy

Power of Fire

Power of Magic

Power of Blood

Pacts & Promises

Bonds

Reverse Harem Escapes – Great for a Quick Roll in the Hay with None of the Guilt

Fated Shifter Mates

Mated to the Pack

Mated to Team Shadow

Mated to the Pride

Taming Her Bears

Mated to the Clan

Protected by the Pack

Claimed by the Pack

The Descendants :

Desired by Four

Fate of Three

Shared by the Four

Mates & Magic

The Sharing Spell

The Spell's Price

Backfired Magic